P9-DXN-736

Gunman's Rhapsody

Also by Robert B. Parker

Gunman's

Rhapsody

Robert B. Parker

G. P. PUTNAM'S SONS

NEW YORK

This book is a work of fiction. Names, characters, places,
and incidents are either the product of the author's imagination
or are used fictitiously, and any resemblance to actual persons,
living or dead, business establishments, events, or locales
is entirely coincidental.

G. P. Putnam's Sons
Publishers Since 1838
a member of
Penguin Putnam Inc.
375 Hudson Street
New York, NY 10014

Copyright © 2001 by Robert B. Parker
All rights reserved. This book, or parts thereof, may not
be reproduced in any form without permission.
Published simultaneously in Canada

Library of Congress Cataloging-in-Publication Data

Parker, Robert B., date.
Gunman's rhapsody / Robert B. Parker
p.   cm.
ISBN 0-399-14762-4
1. Earp, Wyatt, 1848–1929—Fiction.   2. United States
marshals—Fiction.   3. Dodge City (Kan.)—Fiction.
PS3566.A686 G86   2001   00-053327
813'.54—dc21

Printed in the United States of America
1   3   5   7   9   10   8   6   4   2

This book is printed on acid-free paper. ∞

BOOK DESIGN BY VICTORIA KUSKOWSKI

Joan: So many towers, so little time

Was this the face that launched a thousand ships

And burned the topless towers of Ilium? Helen, make me

immortal with a kiss . . .

MARLOWE, *Faust*

Gunman's Rhapsody

Prologue

He already had a history by the time he first saw her, a reputation made in Kansas. He was already a figure of the dime novels, and he already half believed in the myth of the gunman that he was creating even as it created him. He wasn't merely Virgil's brother. He was the man who stood down Clay Allison in Dodge City.

He'd come to Dodge by way of Ellsworth and Wichita from the buffalo camps where every day he shot two buffalo a minute with a breechloading .52-caliber Sharps rifle. Set the shooting stick, rest the Sharps, aim at one, almost any one, among the vast flood of ill-contrived animals and fire. The herd paid no attention to the down animal or to the gunshot. Fire again. Litter the Kansas prairie with the carcasses of the limitless buffalo. Cartridges cost a quarter. Buffalo hides sold for three dollars apiece, to be processed into rakish coats and warm robes for people who had never seen a buffalo, or into steam gaskets and traction belts that powered the machines of eastern industry. The skinners would make their cuts, tie the hide to a rope, turn the rope around a saddle horn, spur the horse and tear the hide from the carcass. Sometimes the cook would cut a tongue or a liver or a roast from the hump. But there were far too many to eat, and most of them were left to rot under the high Kansas sky. The stench of the rotting meat infested the plain and clung to the hunters and skinners, so that, in town, the whores would turn their heads away. It was the stench that finally drove him from it. He liked the gun work because he liked guns. They were balanced and complete and efficient and tightly integrated and purposeful. He liked shooting guns because he was good at it and because it was so complete an act. See something, aim at it, fire the gun, kill the something. There was always closure to a gun. And he didn't mind the camps. He liked the company of other men who liked guns. He liked the rare meat and strong coffee and the rhythm of the day's shooting. He liked the sense of space and possibility at night with the vast overlay of sky promising measureless likelihood. He didn't mind the killing. It was part of the rhythm of life as he understood it. But he didn't like the long, slow conflagration of death, its stench drifting invisibly from the degenerating corpses. So finally he sold the Sharps to Bat Masterson, wrapped his clothes and money in his bedroll, strapped the bedroll behind his saddle and rode his blue roan gelding northeast with an 1873 Army Colt stuck in his belt.

He was an assistant city marshal in Dodge when he met Clay Allison on Front Street at the time of early evening when the sun has set but it's still light and the air has a bluish tinge to it.

"You know me?" Allison said.

"Yes."

"You the fella shot Georgie Hoy?" Allison said.

"Yes."

"You heeled?"

He opened his coat and let Allison see the Colt for which the city had bought him a holster. Allison looked at the gun for a moment.

"Next time I see you I'm going to kill you," Allison said.

"Maybe."

The two men stood close together in silence. He could almost feel the evening deepening.

"You ain't afraid of me much, are you?" Allison said.

"Not much."

Allison nodded as if to himself.

"You will be," Allison said.

Allison turned and started to walk away and stopped. Ten feet behind him and off to his right was a double-barreled, 10-gauge shotgun, the kind that Wells Fargo issued. Holding it steady on him with both hammers back was a young man who looked a lot like the city marshal he'd just braced.

"My brother," the city marshal said behind him. "Morgan."

Allison turned back and looked into the marshal's Colt held straight out at shoulder level, pointed directly at his face.

"I'll take your gun," the marshal said. "Give it back when you leave."

Allison stood motionless for a moment, looking at the marshal.

"You ain't got the stuff to face me even up?" Allison said.

"No point to it when I don't have to. Take the gun out really slow and put it on the ground."

Allison studied the marshal's face beyond the bottomless eye of the gun barrel. There was nothing to see in it. The marshal's gaze was as focused and blank as the Colt that he held steady on Allison's face. Allison took the .45 out of his belt, holding it with his hands on the cylinder, and bent forward and placed it on the unpaved street between them. Then he straightened as slowly as he had bent forward, and smiled.

"You don't give a goddamn," Allison said.

The marshal kicked the Colt away from them over toward the boardwalk in front of the St. James Saloon. His brother picked it up.

"You'd kill me and not mind it a little bit," Allison said.

Without comment the marshal walked over, took the gun from his brother, and stuck it in his belt. Allison nodded, smiling more broadly.

"Hell, you wouldn't mind all that much if I killed you," Allison said.

"How do you know?" he said.

"Because you're like me, is how I know," Allison said. "Dying don't mean shit to you, even if it's you."

He told Allison he could get his gun back on the way out of town, but Allison left in the morning without it, so the marshal sold Allison's gun to a gunsmith and gave half the money to his brother. He never saw Clay Allison again, but he thought of him often, though he never spoke of it to his brothers or to Mattie, who lived with him and called herself his wife.

In the winter of 1879, Dodge had lost its snap. Age thirty-one, he loaded Mattie and all they owned in a wagon, and went with two of his brothers and their women to Tombstone, Arizona, where the silver mines were.

He was there only three days when a show came to town from San Francisco. He went to see it. When he got into his seat and the curtain went up, all he could look at was one girl in the chorus. It was her face most of all. Framed in thick black hair, bright with stage makeup, hot in the gaslights, it burned into his center self and stayed there unchanged by time for the rest of his life. The eyes were very big and dark. The nose was straight, the mouth was wide. Her body in its revealing costume was opulent, and he was not dismissive of it. But her face seemed to him like the face of a god dancing in the chorus of *Pinafore on Wheels*. He went backstage afterward, but it was the troupe's last night in Tombstone and they were already striking the flimsy set and packing the shabby costumes. In the busyness of departure, he missed her and shrugged and left the theater.

5

Her name was Josie Marcus. He would remember it. He didn't know if he would ever see her again, but he would remember her name and if he did see her again, he would be ready. In the months that followed, he still thought about Clay Allison. He wondered how much alike they really were. A lot of people thought Clay was crazy. Clay was supposed to have cut someone's head off in El Paso. He knew he wasn't crazy, the way Clay was supposed to be. He knew he was more like Virgil, who simply went straight ahead, without hesitation, and did whatever had to be done, without comment. But what Allison had said was something to think about, and he went back to it quite often. As he settled into Tombstone, however, he thought about it less. More and more he thought about being ready for Josie Marcus. And after a while Clay Allison faded and he thought about Josie Marcus nearly all the time.

One

The road from the railhead in Benson ended with an uphill pull into Tombstone, and the horses were always lathered as they reached level ground and finished the trip on Allen Street in front of Wells Fargo. They were blowing hard when Bud Philpot tied the reins around the brake handle and climbed down to help the passengers out. Wyatt stayed up on the box holding the double-barreled 10-gauge shotgun that the company issued to all its messengers for the stage run. The in-town guards were issued twelves. When the money box was on the ground, Wyatt climbed down after it and followed as Philpot carried it into the office. Since he'd hired on as a shotgun messenger there had been no holdups, and when there had been holdups, before he took the job, they had always taken place on the road. Still, he saw little sense in being ready for no holdups, so he forced himself always to assume that one was about to happen.

Wyatt rode the empty stage with Philpot on around to Sandy Bob's barn on the corner of Third Street. Then he got down and walked a block down to Fremont, where he and his brothers had been building houses. There were four of the houses done, including the one he lived in with Mattie, and another one under way.

Virgil was there with Allie, sitting at the kitchen table drinking coffee. Virgil was five years older and a little thicker than Wyatt, but they looked alike and people sometimes mistook Wyatt for his brother. He was always pleased when they did.

"Thank God," Mattie said when he came into the kitchen.

She had on a high-necked dress and her hair was tight around her square face. Her cheekbones smudged with a red flush made her look a little feverish. Probably whiskey. Whiskey made her lively. Laudanum made her languid.

"Safe at last," he said.

"Don't laugh at me, Wyatt," Mattie said. "You know about Victorio leaving the reservation."

"I heard," Wyatt said. "But I didn't see him on the road from Benson."

"Oh, leave her be, Wyatt, you know the Apaches are real," Allie said. "People are coming in from Dragoon."

"That so, Virg?"

Virgil nodded. He held his coffee cup in both hands, elbows on the table, so that he had only to dip his head forward to drink some.

"Everybody in Tombstone's worried. There's talk they'll attack the town," Mattie said.

8

She spoke in a kind of singsong, like a girl telling someone her lesson.

Wyatt broke the shotgun, took out the shells and put them in his pocket. He closed the shotgun and leaned its muzzle up against the door frame.

"How many Apaches are out?" Wyatt said.

"Clum says 'bout fifty."

"How many armed men we got in Tombstone?" Wyatt said.

Virgil dipped his head forward and drank some coffee.

"More 'n fifty," he said.

Wyatt nodded absently, looking past Mattie out the back window at the scrub growth and shaled gravel that spilled down the slope behind the house.

"Well, I'm glad you're home safe," Mattie said and got up and walked to him and put her arms around him. He stood quietly while she did this. And when she put her face up he kissed her without much emphasis.

"Go down the Oriental, Virg? Play a couple hands?"

Virgil nodded. He put down his cup, stood up, took his hat off the table and put it on his head. Allie frowned at Virgil.

"Maybe we'll just come along," Allie said. "Me and Mattie. See what the high life looks like."

"No," Virgil said.

"Why not?"

"No place for ladies."

"Ladies?" Allie said. "When did we get to be ladies?"

"Since you married us," Wyatt said and opened the door.

"I didn't marry no 'us,'" Allie said. "I married Virgil."

Virgil grinned at her and took hold of her nose and gave it a little wiggle.

"And a goddamned good thing you did," he said.

Then he went out the door after Wyatt.

They walked a block up to Allen Street. It was winter, and cold for the desert with the threat of snow making the air seem more like it had seemed in Illinois before a blizzard.

"Kinda hard on Mattie," Virgil said.

"I know."

"She's doing the best she can," Virgil said.

"So am I."

They walked along Allen Street. You could see the breath of the horses tied in front of the saloons. The early evening swirl of cowboys and miners moved hurriedly, wrapped in big coats, hunched against the cold.

"She ain't much," Virgil said.

"No," Wyatt said, "she ain't."

"Still, you took up with her."

"Yep."

Virgil put his left hand on Wyatt's shoulder for a moment, then they pushed into the Oriental where it was warm and bright and noisy.

Two

He liked saloons. He liked the easy pace of them, the way the light filtered in through the swinging doors and profiled the dust motes hanging in the still air. In winter he liked the warmth from the coal stove and the mass of men. In summer he liked the way the half-dark room was cooler than the desert heat. He liked the smell of beer, and the card games, and the sense of oneness with the men who, like himself, liked saloons. He liked the lazy undercurrent of trouble that always murmured just below the surface of things.

The only women who came to the saloons were whores. He liked the whores with their easy manner. Sometimes he went to a room with one. Sex aside, they seemed more like men to him, men who let things come to them and didn't fret. There was comfort in a saloon, and possibility, and he liked to lounge at a table sipping coffee, and size up things as he rolled prospects around in his head. He always drank coffee, or root beer. Whiskey made him feel sick. One glass made him dizzy.

Virgil had beer.

"Mistuh Earp."

He knew the voice with its soft Georgia drawl slurring the r's. And as always when he heard the voice he felt a small flicker of excitement. The voice was trouble.

"John Henry," he said without turning around.

The speaker was very thin with ash-blond hair. He stepped around from behind him and hitched a chair and sat at the table. There was something citified about him, something in the graceful way he moved that seemed out of place in the boisterous saloon. He was holding a glass of whiskey.

"Virgil," he said.

"Doc."

"You boys working or just enjoying the atmosphere?"

"Enjoying," Wyatt said.

"How's Mattie?" Doc said.

His eyes were restless as he talked, always moving, looking at the room, looking at everyone, never settling on anything.

Wyatt shrugged.

"You still trailing Big-Nose Kate along?" Virgil said.

Doc laughed.

"A man will do a lot for a small dose of free poontang," he said. "Look at your brother."

"That's not Wyatt's problem," Virgil said.

"No? So what is it? A weakness for hopheads?"

Wyatt looked at Holliday silently, and for a moment Doc saw what Clay Allison had seen on the street in Dodge.

"No offense, Wyatt. You know me. I'm a drunk. I say anything."

"No offense, Doc."

"But how come you stay with Mattie, Wyatt? Hell, you don't even like her."

"We all got women," Wyatt said.

"And you don't want to be the only one," Doc said.

"I brought her down here," Wyatt said. "She wouldn't get along well on her own."

Doc looked at Virgil.

"You understand your brother?" he said.

Virgil smiled slowly.

"Yeah," he said. "I guess I do."

Doc shrugged and shook his head. He went to drink and realized his glass was empty. He stood.

"Be right back," he said. "You boys want anything?"

Both Earps said no. At the bar, Doc got two glasses of whiskey. As he turned from the bar, a big man in a black jacket with velvet lapels jostled him and Doc spilled one of the drinks onto the triangle of white shirt that showed above the last button of the black coat.

"You better be careful what you're doing, skinny," the man in the black coat said.

Doc stared at him for half a second and then threw the

other drink into his face, glass and all. In a continuation of the gesture his hand continued on under his own coat and came out with a short silver Smith & Wesson revolver. He thumbed the hammer back as he drew the gun.

"Are you ready to die today?" Doc said.

There were red smudges on his cheekbones and his voice was high and metallic. He held the gun straight on the big man's face.

The big man wiped the whiskey from his face and stared at Doc's gun.

"You scrawny little bastard," he said. "I ought to take that thing 'way from you and wring your goddamned neck."

"Do it." Doc's voice had dropped to a shrill whisper. "Go ahead and do it, you sonova bitch."

The space around the two men had cleared; one of the bartenders leaned across the bar and spoke to Doc.

"No sense to this, Doc, it was just an accident."

Without taking his eyes off the big man, Doc swatted at the bartender with the back of his left hand. The bartender pulled his head back out of the way. Wyatt and Virgil got up from their table and walked over. They reached Doc at about the time the owner of the Oriental, Bill Joyce, appeared around the end of the bar.

"Goddammit, Doc," Joyce shouted.

"You can be next," Doc said.

The big man wasn't backing down. He kept staring at Doc, his hand lingering close to his right hip.

Wyatt stepped in front of Doc, and Virgil stepped in close against the big man, pressing his own hip against the big man's right hip.

"Enough," Wyatt said. "Enough."

"Get out of the way, Wyatt."

Wyatt shook his head and with the palm of his open left hand gently pushed Doc's gun away from the big man and up so that it pointed toward the pressed-tin ceiling of the bar. Then he closed his hand around the gun with two fingers between the hammer and the cartridge. They stood motionless for a moment in that posture and then Doc slowly opened his hand and Wyatt took the gun. He eased the hammer down and handed it to the bartender, who stowed it behind the bar.

Looking at the big man in the black coat across Wyatt's shoulder, Doc said, "What's your name?"

"John Tyler," the big man said. "You better remember it."

Doc smiled. "What'd you say it was?"

The two men looked at each other for another moment, each restrained by an Earp, then Tyler shrugged and turned and left the bar. He shrugged the collar up on his black coat and went outside without looking back. There was a brief surge of cold air as he opened the door and went out onto Allen Street.

By the time they got Doc back to the table the red smudge on his cheekbones had faded and the shrillness had left his voice. Bill Joyce sent him two fresh drinks. Doc picked up a glass of whiskey and held it up to the light. He examined it closely and smiled and nodded his head and drank it and put the empty glass down. Virgil had a sip of beer. Wyatt drank some coffee.

"Ought to drink more whiskey, Wyatt," Doc said. "It's very liberating."

"Be liberating you right out of this world, one of these days," Virgil said.

"Worse ways to go," Doc said and drank from the other glass.

Three

Before he went to bed Wyatt put some wood into the big iron stove in the parlor. He left the bedroom door open so that the heat would spread. He put his revolver on the floor beside his bed and got in under the heavy quilt where Mattie lay on her back. He could smell the whiskey on her breath. As he settled in, she turned away from him on her side, her back to him. He didn't mind. He felt no desire. When he was with her he felt leaden.

Helps keep the bed warm, he thought. Good for something.

She'd been fun once. A good-natured whore with an easy temperament when he'd met her in Dodge. His brothers had women with them, and Mattie Blaylock was eager to accommodate the man who'd run Clay Allison. But the fun had been mostly saloon fun. At home ironing his shirts, Mattie had lost much of the brightness that had gleamed in the gaslit cheer of the Long Branch. In truth, he realized, much of the brightness and the good nature had come from alcohol, and, domesticated, she could no longer consume enough of it, even boosted with laudanum, to be much more than the petulant slattern that was probably who she really was. Still, she could cook and her sewing brought in some money. And he didn't have to spend much time with her. His brothers were here. There were prospects in Tombstone. There was money to be made. And he could use up most of his time trying to make it. Only at night did he feel loss, at night, or in those moments when she tried to make of their situation something more than it was. He hated her attempts to be affectionate, and he hated much worse her attempts to elicit affection from him. If she would merely provide him the domestic service he needed, he would ask for little more. A man needed a woman at home. Virgil had Allie, whom he considered a mouthy little bitch, but Virgil liked her. James and Jessie, Morgan and Lou, Wyatt and Mattie. He made a face in the cold darkness. Still, there was a symmetry to it, all the Earps, all their women. He thought about Josie Marcus with the big dark eyes whom he'd seen on stage. He knew she would be different. He felt his throat thicken, and the center of himself fold inward. He felt Mattie's backside pressed against his under the comforter. He inched away, so that there was space between them, and thought no more of Josie Marcus, and lay leaden until he fell asleep.

Four

In July, Charlie Shibell, who was the Pima county sheriff, came over from Tucson and they ate antelope steaks, beans, and biscuits in the Can Can.

"Need a deputy," Shibell said. "You got the background and I hear you got the temperament. You want the job?"

"How much?" Wyatt said.

"Pay ain't the thing," Shibell said. "Part of the job is to collect taxes; most of it's easy collection—mining companies and the railroad. You keep a percentage."

"Of everything I collect?"

"Yep."

"Got to shoot anybody?"

"Not so often," Shibell said. "When you do, you give me a voucher for the ammunition."

"I got to keep regular hours?" Wyatt said.

"You mean, go to the jail and sit there every day? Hell no. You get them taxes collected, we'll be happy over in Tucson."

"I'm your man," Wyatt said.

An hour later, with a star on his shirt, he walked up Allen Street to Vronan's bowling alley, where his brother James tended bar. Wyatt had a badge again, like Virgil.

Behind the bar James poured his younger brother some coffee. He did it with his left hand. Wyatt knew he did almost everything with his left hand. He had taken a Rebel miniball in his right shoulder at Sharpsburg. And eighteen years later, his right arm still wasn't much use. He could use it as a kind of support for his left hand, and he had learned to compensate so that most people didn't notice that he was mostly one-handed until they had gotten to know him well.

"Morgan will want one too," James said.

"He can do special deputy work for us," Wyatt said.

"Virgil gets to be city marshal," James said, "be a lot of special deputy work."

Wyatt grinned.

"Better send for Warren," he said. "Be work for all of us."

Jim shook his head.

"Not my kind of work."

"Got plenty of Earps for shooting," Wyatt said. "We need you to manage our affairs."

"Soon as we get some," James said.

"We're building the houses," Wyatt said. "Some of our mining claims could work. We make some money dealing cards. Virgil's a deputy marshal, and now I got this tax-collecting job and Virgil's going to run for city marshal. Morgan got his shotgun work for Wells Fargo. And he and I do some private work for them, too. Things are looking up for the Earp brothers."

"In a little while," James said, "they'll probably be changing the name of this place to Earpstone."

Wyatt smiled. He was holding his coffee cup in both hands, as if to warm them. When he drank he raised the cup only slightly and sipped by dipping his head down to it, his eyes moving slowly as he looked about him. Always on the lookout, James thought. All the time looking for the main chance.

"Things are looking up," Wyatt said, "for the Earp brothers."

He drank again from his coffee cup, his eyes looking out over the rim at the few miners who were bowling at midday, at the rough bar, at the door that opened onto Allen Street, looking at everything there was to see . . . and more.

Five

"You got no goddamned right rummaging around in my shed," Frank McLaury said to Virgil Earp.

"Tracked them Army mules to here, Frank."

Virgil was dismounted, holding a running iron he'd picked up from among the McLaury irons in the shed. Behind him, still mounted, were Wyatt and Morgan. To their right was an Army lieutenant named Hurst and a cavalry squad from Camp Rucker.

"You see any mules, Virgil?"

Behind Frank was his brother Tom and a group of cowhands, most of them armed. His neighbor Frank Patterson stood with Tom, though he showed no weapon.

"They had 'U S' on their shoulders, Frank. What'd you change it to? Something with an eight in it? Every damn rustler in Arizona changes an S to an eight."

"You calling me a rustler, you sonova bitch?"

Virgil shifted the running iron to his left hand. Wyatt kicked his feet free of the stirrups so he could go fast off the horse to his left and keep it between him and the cowboys. To his right he could see Morgan smiling. Morgan loved trouble.

"Frank," Patterson said to McLaury, "let's you and me just step over here and talk with the lieutenant."

"My name's known all over the goddamned state," McLaury said. His face was red. His eyes seemed large. He had a mustache and a tricky little goatee that Wyatt thought made him look foolish.

"Sure it is," Patterson said. "And everybody knows you're dead honest. No point making a fight over nothing. Let's talk with the lieutenant."

"Go ahead, Frank. No need for trouble," Tom McLaury said. "Talk with the lieutenant."

With a hand on McLaury's arm, Patterson moved him away from the Earps, past the cavalry squad, and into the thin shade of a single mesquite tree.

"Hey, Virg," Morgan said. "I'm betting he run the 'U S' into a D eight."

Virgil smiled slightly and didn't answer.

"Am I right?" Morgan said to the cowboys. "I mean, what else you going to make it into?"

"Could be an O eight," Wyatt said.

They were facing west, into the sun, and Wyatt had his hat tipped forward so that the brim shadowed his eyes. He would not have chosen this position. He'd have liked the sun behind him, in their eyes. But you didn't always get to choose. Especially with Virgil. When Virgil went at something, he went straight at it and didn't maneuver much.

"Or maybe a 'Q B,' " Morgan said. "You think these cowboys are smart enough to make a 'U S' into a 'Q B'?"

"You boys quiet down," Virgil said, without taking his eyes off the cowboys. "We're just after some stolen mules. Don't need to get these fellas all riled up about whether they're smart or not."

Morgan grinned.

"Just passing time, Virg."

"Well, pass it quiet."

Morgan grinned again. He sat silently astride his big chestnut horse, lightly rubbing the fingertips of his right hand slowly up and down his shirtfront. Everyone was silent, facing each other in the hot dirt yard of the ranch. One of the Army horses snorted and tossed his head to clear a fly. It made his harness creak, and some of the hardware jangled briefly. Then it was silent again. There was no wind, and the desert smell mingled with the smell of horses.

Lieutenant Hurst rode back from the mesquite tree alone. Patterson and McLaury stayed there watching.

"We won't be needing you boys anymore," Hurst said. "Patterson knows where the mules are."

"And he'll show you where they are if you send us away and nobody gets arrested," Virgil said.

Hurst smiled, and shrugged.

"Guess we don't need evidence," Virgil said and dropped the running iron he'd been holding.

He swung up into his saddle. Wyatt slipped his feet back into his stirrups.

"No arrests?" Virgil said.

"No," Hurst said.

"Your mules," Virgil said and turned his horse and nodded to his brothers.

"My brother ain't going to forget you called him a rustler," Tom McLaury said.

Virgil didn't answer. In fact, he showed no sign that he'd heard McLaury. He nudged his horse forward and led out from the McLaury ranch at a walk. Wyatt turned after him. Morgan was the last to leave, and as he rode past the cavalry squad and their lieutenant, he turned back toward the cowboys and leveled his forefinger at them.

"Bang," he said.

Then he laughed and kicked his horse into a trot to catch up with his brothers.

Six

On the ride east to Tombstone, the sun was behind them, so that they were continually riding into their own shadows. They stuck to the rutted wagon road. The desert on either side was dense with brittlebush. There was no hurry, and the horses were allowed to shuffle along. They knew they were headed home. They knew when they got there they'd eat. No need to pay them much attention.

"Morg," Virgil said, "being as how we're the law, we are kind of supposed to stop trouble, not start it."

"Oh hell, Virg," Morgan said, "I was just ragging the cowboys a little. Wyatt was doing it."

"The thing is," Virgil said, "some of those cowboys, you rag 'em too much they are going to try and shoot you."

"Against the three of us? Virg, we'd fan those cowboys before they ever got the hammer back."

"Probably," Virgil said.

Virgil's horse slowed and snorted. The other two skittered sideways, as a snake slid across the road through the dust in front of them.

"Rattler?" Morgan said.

"Bull snake," Wyatt answered.

The horses settled back into their easy walk.

" 'Course, there's no special reason to fan them cowboys," Virgil said.

"If they pulled on us . . ."

"No special reason to push them into pulling on us," Virgil said.

Morgan shrugged. He was riding between Virgil and Wyatt. Like always, Wyatt was watching the horizon, looking at the landscape, surveying the snakeweed and squawberry. Wyatt heard the conversation, Morgan knew. Wyatt heard everything. But he was, as he almost always was, not quite there. Always there was space around Wyatt.

"Killing don't usually end things," Virgil said. "Sometimes it just starts things rolling. Sometimes you got to shoot, and when you got to you best be quick about it. But it's better when you don't got to."

"Feels like I'm still home listening to Papa," Morgan said.

"You never paid much attention to him either," Virgil said.

Morgan laughed.

"Be glad when Warren gets here," Morgan said. "Then I can lecture him."

They reached Tombstone at sunset, and rode up the hill and onto Allen Street as the sun was just at horizon level and their shadows stretched before them in angular distortion. At the corner of Fourth Street, Wyatt saw Josie Marcus coming out of Solomon's bank with Johnny Behan, who owned a livery stable with a man named Dunbar. Wyatt didn't know Behan very well. But Behan was a Democrat, which didn't sit well with any of the Earps. He was also a smooth-talking, fancy-Dan kind of man. Wyatt was pretty sure if he knew him better he wouldn't like him. Behan and Josie turned right on the plank sidewalk and walked east along Allen Street past the Oriental. Wyatt said nothing. His horse continued to plod unguided along Allen Street. Under the hat brim Wyatt's eyes steadied and held on the woman walking ahead of him. He seemed to relax into the saddle, his hands resting on the pommel. At Fifth Street the horses turned left, heading toward Bullock and Crabtree's Livery, where they boarded. Wyatt's horse, responding to some pressure neither Morgan nor Virgil could see, slowed and loitered for a moment. Josie Marcus continued up Allen Street beside Behan, her hips swaying only slightly, her head perfectly still. She walked like a lady. Halfway up the block she went, with Behan, into Hartman's Jewelry. When she had disappeared, Wyatt's horse turned, and followed the other horses down Fifth Street. Wyatt didn't look back, nor did he speak of it to his brothers. But when he'd turned the horse over to the boy at the livery, and his brothers headed home down Fremont Street, he didn't go with them. Instead, he walked up to the Oriental and got a cup of coffee and went to a corner table by himself and sat facing the door, sipping his coffee, holding the cup in both hands, and looking out through the door at Allen Street.

CHRONICLE

SURVEY:

British troops defeat the Zulus at Ulundi . . . Alsace Lorraine comes under German rule . . . Dostoyevsky's *Brothers Karamazov* is published . . . The electric light bulb is developed by Thomas Edison . . . Emile Zola publishes *Nana* . . . James Garfield elected twentieth President . . . In New York City, Sarah Bernhardt makes her first American appearance . . . Lew Wallace publishes *Ben Hur* . . . Swiss writer Johanna Spyri publishes *Heidi* . . . The population of the United States reaches Fifty Million . . . Offenbach's *Tales of Hoffman* is produced.

* * *

Cheyenne, Wyoming, October 25—

A well informed merchent from Green River, who arrived here on business, brings further particulars of the Indian scare in Southern Utah, and Western Wyoming. In regard to the Sintah-Utes and Snakes being on the war path, he says Washakies' band of Snakes were never more peaceable, except a few ringleaders who stole some horses and cattle on Brusby Creek and Ashley Fork, and thus created all the excitement.

* * *

Washington, October 25—

The following was received at the Indian bureau this evening.

Los Pinos, October 21

Arrived at 2 p.m. Everything quiet at present. Had a talk with Ouray, and with two couriers just arrived from a hostile camp fifteen miles this side of Grand River, about halfway between here and White River Agency. Mrs. Meeker, Miss Meeker, Mrs. Price, and her two children are prisoners in Johnson's camp. The couriers met General Adams last night, one day's march from the hostile camp. Ouray believes the prisoners will be delivered to General Adams . . .

Pollock, Inspector

* * *

Washington, October 25—

General Meyer, Chief of the Signal Service, has submitted his annual report. He says 170 stations have been maintained during the year to fill the system of observation from which reports are deemed necessary to enable proper warning to be given of the approach and force of storms and of other meteoric changes for the benefit of agricultural and commercial interest.

* * *

Washington, October 25—

In a report to the Secretary of the Navy, concerning affairs in Samoa, Commander Chandler who was sent to the Island to protect American Interests, says that the condition of affairs is very complicated. There are three governments, so called—one old government party, occupying a portion of the territory, and another, opposition, occupying another portion, and the government of British, American, and German consuls over the territorial portions. Captain Chandler has succeeded in protecting many American interests, though obstacles have had to be overcome. He understood that the old government party which was once virtually overthrown, and the opposition, which to some extent succeeded, were going to war again. He has stated publicly that he will recognize neither, but will protect American interests. He also understands that a British man-of-war, commanded by the plenipotentiary, was on its way to establish a British protectorate over the island. In this case he would protest against Pago-Pago, which has been ceded by treaty with Samoa to the United States, being occupied and would proceed there to protect the station. It is a very important position, he says, for a cooling station, and recommends that it be at once occupied by the United States as such.

* * *

London, October 25—

A Capetown dispatch states that the Boers, the original Dutch settlers of South Africa, who have never submitted with good grace to British rule, have, since the conclusion of the Zulu war and the occupation of a larger portion than ever of the country, shows (*sic*) increasing dissatisfaction with the situation, and they are now actively engaged in fomenting disturbances.

* * *

New Bedford, October 25—

In Fall River today, the first ball game for the championship for Fall River and New Bedford took place. On the last half of the ninth inning, Fall River being at bat, Umpire Ryan of Fall River called the game on account of darkness, setting it back to the eighth inning as a tie.

INNINGS	1	2	3	4	5	6	7	8	9	
NEW BEDFORD	1	0	3	0	0	0	1	6	4	—15
FALL RIVER	1	0	3	2	0	2	0	3	3	—14

Errors—Fall River 14; New Bedford 134; Base hits—Each, 12.

* * *

EXPORTATION OF CATTLE—

Most everybody has a vague idea, at least, that the exportation of cattle to foreign countries is a business of considerable importance and magnitude, and one that is constantly growing in extent. Cattle raising on the western plains is now recognized as a specific industry and one that bids fair to increase in volume and become an important factor in the trade between the old world and the new. Hundreds of young men have left comfortable homes in the east, for the west, to engage in it, being able and willing to "rough it," as the saying is, and buffet the hardships of the prairie in hopes of obtaining a competency.

* * *

"BUCKS" AT THEIR TOILET—

The gigantic warriors of the Osage tribe, who realize one's ideal of the typical Indian, decorate their person in the highest style of barbaric art. Painting their faces in the prevailing fashion of the tribe was the first thing done, and took precedence of every other matter of dress. As a consequence of this reversed order of things, the herculean Osage brave stalked about before the high heaven, clad only in a calico of an abbreviated pattern, and perfectly nude as to the remainder of his body.

* * *

LADIES
We have a large job lot of Ladies ALL WOOL Scarlet underwear at $1.45, which we find is a much better quality, than anything else in Boston for $1.50. RAYMOND & CO. 6 and 8 Tremont St.

* * *

GUNS
2000 nearly new UNITED STATES RIFLES (small caliber) $1.75 each.
In lots of 20 or upwards $1.50 each.
Sent by express, C.O.D. if desired

A. D. PUFFER & Sons
46 & 48 Portland St.

Seven

Behind his house, down the slope, maybe half a mile, amidst the hardscrabble desert scrub, Wyatt stood and fired at an old whiskey barrel set upon a rock. He had drawn a target on it, and several times a week he would walk down there and fire at it. First from ten yards. Then twenty, then fifty. If you were shooting at someone beyond fifty yards, with a handgun, in Virgil's phrase, you might do better to call him names. It was his second barrel, the first one having been, finally, shot to pieces. He used a single-action Colt .45 with a walnut handle. Wyatt liked to shoot. He liked the control. He liked the sudden expansion of energy when he fired and the Colt didn't so much buck as levitate slightly, as if the restraint of gravity were momentarily removed. He fired five rounds, sighting carefully each time. He'd known for a long time that accurate was more important than quick. Then he flipped open the cylinder, ejected the spent shells, and loaded five fresh rounds, leaving the chamber empty under the hammer. He moved back ten yards and fired carefully again.

It wasn't until he finished firing that he was aware of Mattie.

"Wyatt," she said.

He looked around at her, as if he were waking from a light sleep. His hands were already unloading and reloading, taking the thick Remington cartridges from a tin box that said ".45 Colt" on it, and, in smaller letters, "50 Central Fire Cartridges."

"Milt Joyce is looking for you," Mattie said. "He came by and asked if you'd stop in and see him."

"All right," Wyatt said.

"What do you suppose he wants?" Mattie said.

"When I stop by," Wyatt said, "I'll ask him."

"Ain't he on the Democrat side?" Mattie said.

"I guess so," Wyatt said.

He slid the reloaded gun, with an empty chamber under the hammer, into the worn holster he'd brought with him from Dodge. He picked his coat up from the rock where he'd folded and put it on and put the box of cartridges into the side pocket.

"Isn't it awful warm to be wearing a coat, Wyatt?"

"I like to carry my gun," Wyatt said. "But I don't like people seeing me walking around heeled."

"Even though you're a deputy?"

"If I'm going to get somewhere in this town, it don't help if people think I'm a gunman."

Mattie nodded silently. But that's what you are, she thought, that's exactly what you are. But she didn't say it. Wyatt wasn't good at listening to her. He wasn't too good at listening to anyone, except sometimes Virgil. So she followed him silently up the hill, and put out a clean shirt for him to wear when he went to see Mr. Joyce.

When Wyatt went into the Oriental, Milt Joyce came out of his small office at the end of the bar. He stepped behind the bar and took a bottle and two glasses and led Wyatt to a table at the far end of the bar. He set the bottle and glasses on the table and gestured Wyatt toward a seat. Before he himself sat down, he tilted all four chairs at the next table up against the table so no one would sit there. Then he sat next to Wyatt and poured a drink. He gestured toward the second glass and Wyatt shook his head.

"Don't drink, Milt."

"By God, that's right, you don't," Joyce said. "Want some coffee? Soda pop?"

"No, thanks."

"Not so many men around here don't drink," Joyce said.

Wyatt shrugged. Joyce turned his glass in small compass on the table.

"See where you got to be a deputy sheriff," Joyce said.

Wyatt nodded. His hands were folded quietly on top of the table. His body seemed at ease in the straight chair. His white shirt was freshly starched under the dark coat and he was clean-shaven except for a mustache. He looked healthy and strong, Joyce thought.

"Virgil going to run for city marshal?" Joyce said.

"Might," Wyatt said.

There's a lot of space around him, Joyce thought.

"How 'bout you?" Joyce said. "Be interested in buying into the saloon business?"

"Got a faro table 'cross the street," Wyatt said. "At the Eagle."

"You can keep that. I'm talking about a piece of the whole thing."

"Here?"

"Yes. I'm offering to sell you a quarter interest in the Oriental," Joyce said.

"Don't probably have that kind of cash right handy," Wyatt said.

"We could work out a deal in services," Joyce said.

Wyatt sat silently, his hands at peace on the tabletop. Joyce turned his glass some more. For a moment there was no expression on Wyatt's face, and then there was the hint of a smile.

"You having trouble with somebody?" Wyatt said.

Joyce stared into the top of his glass as he turned it on the scuffed tabletop. Then he picked it up and drank half of its contents and put it down. He opened his mouth and let out his breath.

"John Tyler," Joyce said. "Your friend Holliday got into it with him a while back."

"I know him," Wyatt said.

"You know what he does for work?" Joyce said.

"He's a gunhand," Wyatt said.

"He's told people in town that he's going to put me out of business."

"Why?" Wyatt said.

"Doesn't say. My guess is he's been hired by some people who'd like me out of the way so they could take over my customers."

"How's he planning on doing that?" Wyatt said.

"Come in here, talk loud, make trouble. Whiskey is whiskey," Joyce said. "Cards are cards. Lot of other places to get them in this town. Man makes trouble here, people will go where there's no one making trouble."

"And you want me to deal with Tyler."

"Yes."

"And you'll give me a quarter interest."

"Better you get a quarter than Tyler gets it all," Joyce said.

"I expect that would be better," Wyatt said. "On the other hand, you could probably get Doc Holliday to shoot him for nothing."

Joyce shook his head.

"I know he's a friend of yours, Wyatt, but Doc's crazy."

"And you think I'm not," Wyatt said.

"Not like Doc."

Wyatt smiled.

"No," he said. "Not like Doc."

"You game?" Joyce said.

"Our politics are pretty different," Wyatt said.

"This ain't a political deal," Joyce said.

"Suppose it isn't," Wyatt said. "I'll talk with my brother."

"I need a quick answer," Joyce said. "I'm already having trouble with Tyler."

"Let you know tomorrow."

"I guess I can hang on until then," Joyce said.

Wyatt shifted in his chair.

"I'll take that coffee now," he said.

Joyce spoke to the barman, and he brought a cup. Wyatt held it with both hands resting on the table.

"Saw Johnny Behan with a new woman," Wyatt said.

"Yes. He brought her back from Denver."

"I think I saw her last year in a show came through here," Wyatt said. He wasn't looking at Joyce. He was looking disinterestedly around the room, which in the early afternoon was nearly empty.

"Could be," Joyce said. "She's supposed to be some kind of actress."

"Name was Josie something," Wyatt said.

"Marcus," Joyce said. "Josephine Marcus. Jewish. Johnny introduced me to her."

"Nice-looking woman," Wyatt said.

Eight

All of the Earps were there, around a table in Hatch's Saloon. Two cowboys were drinking beer and playing pool behind them, while several of their friends drank beer and watched. The bar was lined nearly solid with a mix of cowboys, miners, and townsmen. At a table near the front four bullwhackers played cards while they waited for their wagons to be loaded. Some whores, dressed for work, were having late breakfast at another table. They looked kind of tired in the daylight, Wyatt thought.

"Be a nice foot in the door at the Oriental," James said. "Frank Joyce is an up-and-comer."

"You know Tyler?" Virgil said.

Wyatt nodded.

"You know his reputation?"

"Gunhand."

Virgil nodded slowly.

"Wyatt's a pretty fair gunhand himself," Morgan said.

"Tyler won't back off," Virgil said. "You go against him, you have to mean it."

"I always mean it," Wyatt said.

"Quarter interest in a place like the Oriental is worth something," James said.

"And we can handle Tyler," Morgan said.

"I think 'we' ain't getting the quarter interest," Virgil said.

"Oh hell, Virg. You know if one of us is in, all of us are in," Morgan said.

As he had at the McLaury ranch, Morgan brushed his gunhand up and down his shirtfront, as if drying the tips of his fingers. Trouble's like a carnival for Morgan, Wyatt thought.

"All of us ain't always going to be around," Virgil said. "You ready to go against Tyler alone, Wyatt?"

"Yes."

"He's a back shooter," Virgil said.

"I'll try to keep him in front of me," Wyatt said.

"I say he takes the offer," Jim said.

"Me too," Morgan said.

"You want to do it, Wyatt?"

"Might as well."

"Well, then I guess you will. No reason to go against Tyler alone, though, if you don't have to. He starts trouble, send for me and Morgan."

Wyatt nodded. His hands rested motionless on the table-top. His eyes moving, as they always were, taking in the room: whores, pool players, drinkers, cardplayers, the sound of glassware, the clink of pool, the smell of whiskey, the economical, practiced movements of the bartender. He liked the rhythm of saloon life very much.

"You do it, Wyatt," James said. "It's why you got brothers."

Wyatt smiled slowly, almost as if his mind were somewhere else and had just refocused.

"Yes," he said. "I know."

Nine

John Behan's white frame house on Third Street had a slant-roofed piazza across the front. There were two straight chairs to the right of the front door. Behan opened the door.

"Wyatt," he said. "Thanks for coming."

Wyatt nodded and stepped into the house. The front room was papered in beige with a European landscape the featured motif. Josie Marcus stood behind Behan, and when he saw her, Wyatt took off his hat.

"This is my fiancée, Wyatt, Miss Josephine Marcus."

"Nice to meet you," Wyatt said. "I remember seeing you in *Pinafore on Wheels* a while back."

"Well, how nice of you to remember," she said. "It wasn't a very big part."

Wyatt didn't say anything. She was aware that his gaze rested on her, and she felt its weight. She noticed at once how tall he was, taller than Johnny, who was regarded as tall, with a hard look of muscle to him, harder than Johnny, and much quieter. Johnny was a talker. This one was not. This one was quiet to his soul, she thought. And, perhaps, quite dangerous.

"Sit down, my friend," Behan said. "Josie, maybe you could make us some coffee."

There were four upholstered chairs with wooden arms in the front room. Josie went to the kitchen; Wyatt sat in one of the upholstered chairs. Behan sat in another one. There was a small oak table with claw-and-ball feet between them, and through the front window they could see out onto Third Street.

"Wyatt, why I wanted to talk with you was about the deputy sheriff's job."

Wyatt waited. A Wells Fargo stage, the horses lathered from the uphill pull into town, went by on the way to Sandy Bob's. Morgan sat up front beside the driver, one foot cocked on top of the floor rail, the trail-issue shotgun in his lap.

"Been talking to Charlie Shibell," Behan said. "Maybe you know this already, but they're thinking that Pima's too big to be one county. So they're going to keep half of it like it is, and make the other half, including Tombstone, into Cochise County."

"I heard that," Wyatt said.

"Well, that will mean a new sheriff, and Charlie and I think it should be a Democrat."

Josie Marcus came back into the front room, carrying a

tray with coffee in three blue and white cups. There was also a bowl of sugar and a small pitcher full of condensed milk. She placed the tray down on the table, took a cup of coffee and seated herself on the couch. Behan looked at her, and for a moment seemed about to say something. But he didn't. Instead he carefully measured three spoonfuls of sugar into his cup and added condensed milk.

"Do you live in town here, Mr. Earp?" Josie said.

"Yes. My brothers and I are building some houses down around the corner on Fremont."

"Well, how nice," she said. "We're neighbors."

"Josie, Wyatt and I are talking a little business."

"Oh, Johnny, you're always talking a little business. I like to know my neighbors. Do you live with your brothers, Mr. Earp?"

"Virgil lives across the street," Wyatt said. "Morgan and James live on either side."

"And who lives in your house, Mr. Earp, besides you?"

"Mattie," Earp said.

Josie Marcus nodded slowly, her great black eyes holding on his, as if what he were saying was more interesting than she could have imagined.

"Your wife," Josie said.

"More or less."

"Josie, if you could just stop talking for maybe a minute or so," Behan said. "I need to ask Wyatt a couple of things."

Josie smiled.

"Of course," she said.

Behan sighed.

"So we was thinking, Charlie and I, that we needed a Democrat to be sheriff of Cochise County."

"So you said."

"And," Behan grinned at Wyatt, "we was thinking that it should be me."

Behan paused for Wyatt to speak. Wyatt didn't speak, and after a moment, Behan continued.

"Thing is, you being a Republican, and a deputy sheriff and all, it might make it a little hard."

The room was warm and still. Wyatt could see Josie studying him as she drank coffee off to his left. She was wearing cologne, and he could smell it from where he sat.

"Can't say as I mind," Wyatt said to Behan.

"Well, no, 'course not. But if you could find your way clear to resigning in favor of me, it would put me in a nice position to be sheriff when the new county comes."

"And why would I do that?"

"Well," and again Behan smiled widely at Wyatt, "I might appoint you under sheriff, if I got appointed."

"Uh-huh."

"And if you resigned in favor of me, then Charlie wouldn't have to fire you."

Watching him, Josie saw no reaction at all. He sat quietly,

holding his coffee cup in both hands. Even when he drank from his coffee cup he was looking at Johnny above the rim. At the same time she knew he was aware of her. She could feel it. His attention was like the heat of a summer afternoon out here. Not emanating from someplace, but all around, enveloping. She liked the feeling.

He sat motionless as if waiting for Johnny to finish. She could see that his silence made Johnny nervous. Many things did. Johnny was a nervous man.

"Charlie said I should tell you that, Wyatt. Nothing personal. Just politics."

Wyatt drank some coffee and put the cup carefully back in its matching saucer. The cups were decorated in blue with pictures of elegant ladies on a lawn.

"I meant what I said, about you being under sheriff."

Wyatt stood and turned politely to Josie Marcus.

"Miss Marcus," he said, "it's been a pleasure to meet you."

"Thank you, Mr. Earp, and a pleasure as well to meet you."

"I hope to see you again," Wyatt said.

His eyes were empty as he spoke. His face had no expression.

Why does that sound so full of sex? she thought.

"I'm sure you will, Mr. Earp. We're neighbors, aren't we?"

"Yes," Wyatt said. "We are."

"What you want me to tell Charlie, Wyatt?"

Wyatt turned his gaze slowly onto Behan and held it.

Then he said, "I don't want you to tell him anything, Johnny." And he turned and, without haste, left the house.

Ten

John Tyler came in out of the late-afternoon glare of August, into the slightly cooler dimness of the Oriental. The early shift was out from the Toughnut, and the room was loud with miners. Tyler was carrying a gun butt forward in front of his left hip. Wyatt was laying out his faro spread, near the back of the long room. He saw Tyler as soon as Tyler came in, and jerked his head at Blonde Marie, one of the whores waiting for business at a table near the piano. She got up and came over.

"Go get my brother," he said.

"Virg?"

"First one you see," Wyatt said.

"Is there going to be trouble?" Blonde Marie said.

"Probably," Wyatt said.

Blonde Marie turned and walked out the front door of the saloon. A blare of sunlight splashed briefly into the saloon as the door opened and swung shut behind her. Wyatt sat quietly behind the faro table, a deck of cards in his hands. Without looking, he cut the cards with one hand and shuffled them and cut them again. He seemed idle. If Tyler saw him, he gave no sign of it. Tyler pushed his way through the miners standing two deep at the bar. He was deliberately rough about it, making no effort to avoid stepping on toes and jostling drinks. Several of the miners looked at him, but no one complained. Tyler ordered whiskey, and when it came he drank it down in a long swallow. Then he turned to a miner next to him, and put his hand flat against the man's face and shoved. The miner staggered and fell backward, landing on the floor in a half-sitting position, catching the rest of his fall with his hands. He was a smallish man with a thick beard, his shoulders strengthened and bowed by labor underground. He seemed more startled than angry as he sat on the floor.

"Hey," he said.

The miner could see the gun Tyler was carrying, and it made him careful.

"You were in my way," Tyler said.

"Hell I was," the miner said.

He got to his feet. His hands were clenched at his sides.

"You saying to me that I'm a liar?" Tyler said.

"I wasn't in your way," the miner said. His eyes kept shifting from Tyler's face to Tyler's gun. "That's all I'm saying."

"And I say you were," Tyler said. "And I say you're in my way right now."

"In your way for what?"

"You know me?" Tyler said.

"Yeah, I know who you are."

"Well, I say you better get out of this saloon now, 'fore I get mad," Tyler said.

"I got a right to be here," the miner said.

"No," Tyler said. "You don't. Not anymore. Go drink someplace else, 'less you want really bad trouble."

"You got no right to push me," the miner said.

"Get out of here now," Tyler said. He let his hand drift downward toward the gun. The miner's friends began to back away, and stubborn though he was, the miner found himself stepping back.

"I don't have no gun," the miner said.

"I do," Tyler said.

"Afternoon, Mr. Tyler," Wyatt said.

He was standing just to Tyler's right and slightly behind him. Tyler wheeled to face him, his shoulders hunching slightly. This was no miner.

"What do you want?" Tyler said.

"Want you to stop causing trouble in my saloon," Wyatt said. He seemed relaxed. His left hand hung quietly by his side. His right rested lightly on his hip, just forward of his holster.

"Your saloon?"

"Quarter interest."

"Don't make you the owner," Tyler said. "Joyce owns the rest."

"You're in my quarter," Wyatt said.

The room was quiet. A wide circle had formed around the two men, and it was in continuous flux as people kept shifting to get out of the line of fire.

"You don't mean nothing to me, Earp."

"I'd like you to leave my saloon," Wyatt said. "Now."

"Don't prod me, Earp."

"Now," Wyatt said.

The silence grew tighter. The front door opened and shut. Neither Tyler nor Wyatt looked at it. Someone whispered, "Here's Virgil." The whisper seemed to take some of the tension out of Tyler. His shoulders sagged.

"That's the way you want it, Earp," he said and turned and started toward the door, where Virgil stood, his eyes adjusting. Tyler bent forward slightly, and his right shoulder tensed. In one smooth gesture Wyatt brought his revolver out from under his coat and hit Tyler across the back of the head with the barrel. Tyler staggered and fell forward, and the gun he'd been pulling spun ahead of him on the wood floor of the saloon. Virgil picked it up. Tyler, on his hands and knees, shook his head trying to clear it, and Wyatt stepped forward and kicked him in the side. Tyler sprawled flat. Wyatt stepped up beside him and put the big Colt against his right temple, finger on the trigger, thumb on the hammer.

"I don't want to see you in my saloon again, Mr. Tyler. You understand?"

Tyler lay facedown, twisted sideways trying to ease the

pain in his side. There was blood seeping through the long black hair at the back of his head. Wyatt banged the muzzle of his revolver against Tyler's temple.

"You understand?"

"Yes," Tyler said hoarsely.

"Good," Wyatt said. "Now get out of my saloon."

Tyler tried to get up, and collapsed back down to his knees. Virgil stuck Tyler's Colt in the pocket of his coat and stepped forward and got hold of the back of Tyler's coat collar, and dragged Tyler to his feet. Wyatt holstered his revolver, then walked past Virgil and opened the front door and held it. The hot light poured in, bringing in with it the strong smell of dust and horses. Virgil half walked, half dragged Tyler into the street. Wyatt closed the door behind them and the room was dim again. He went back to his faro table and examined the layout carefully to make sure it was orderly. At the bar the miners began to talk again. And within moments the surface of saloon life had closed, unruffled, over the incident.

Eleven

It was early September before Wyatt talked with Josie Marcus again. He met her on Fremont Street outside Ward's Market. She was carrying a brown paper bag of groceries.

"May I carry that for you?" Wyatt said.

"Yes you may," Josie said. "And thank you very much, Mr. Earp."

"I'd appreciate it if you'd call me Wyatt."

"If you'll call me Josie."

"Fair swap," Wyatt said. "How've you been enjoying Tombstone, Josie?"

"Well, it certainly is lively, Wyatt."

They both laughed at the self-conscious exchange of first names.

"Johnny talks about you a lot," Josie said. "He's worried about getting to be sheriff."

"How about you, Josie?"

She laughed.

"I don't want to be sheriff."

Wyatt smiled. He looked to her like someone who didn't smile easily or often, so when the smile came it was valuable.

"Would you like it if Johnny were?"

"Johnny says it's a good-paying job."

"I hear it is."

"Then I guess I would like it if Johnny were sheriff."

"Nothing wrong with money," Wyatt said.

"I know," Josie said. "My father has money."

Wyatt was quiet for a time as they stood on the corner of Fourth Street, outside the post office, waiting for a freight wagon to pass, the six big draft horses leaning their mass into the harness.

"You're from San Francisco," Wyatt said.

"Yes."

"And your father has money."

"Yes. Quite a lot."

"So why are you here?"

She smiled up at him. Her mouth was wide. Mattie had a thin mouth that turned down at the corners.

"Looking for adventure," she said.

"With Behan?"

She laughed out loud this time.

"Wyatt, you're speaking of my fiancé," she said.

"I know. I apologize," he said. "But I never thought Behan was much for adventure."

"Well, maybe," Josie said. "He's been a law officer, you know. In Prescott."

Wyatt nodded.

"That's adventurous, isn't it?"

"Uh-huh."

The wagon pulled past. They waited a moment for the dust to settle, and then crossed Fourth Street.

"You've been a law officer in a lot of places."

"Yes," he said. "I have."

Her face was sort of heart-shaped, and her eyes were very large and dark and seemed bottomless to him. When she talked she had none of Mattie's Iowa whine in her voice. In fact, you couldn't tell where she came from by the way she talked. She sounded educated to Wyatt, and the way he assumed upper class would sound. He wasn't sure he'd ever met anybody upper class before. Certainly he'd had little to do with the daughters of rich men.

"My brother Virgil was a constable in Prescott," he said. "I did some teamstering up there for a while."

"Did you or your brother know Johnny?"

"No."

They were quiet then. Walking side by side, Wyatt carrying the groceries, they could have been a domestic couple strolling home from the store.

"I heard you buffaloed John Tyler a while back in the Oriental," Josie said.

"He was making trouble."

"Everyone says he's really dangerous."

Wyatt smiled.

"Maybe they're wrong," he said.

She nodded as if to herself, and tilted her head so she could study him as he walked beside her. Outside of Bauer's butcher shop, across the street from the *Tombstone Epitaph*, Josie stopped. Wyatt stopped with her. She put her hands on her hips and examined his face for a moment. Whatever she was looking for there, she seemed to find.

"You'd be an adventure," she said.

"You think so?"

"Yes," she said. "It's why Johnny worries about you."

"Because I'm an adventure?"

"Because everything's inside," she said. "Everything's under control. You don't hate and you don't love and you don't get mad and you don't get scared. You are a dangerous man, the real thing."

"Maybe I'm not so much like that as you think," he said.

"Oh, I'm sure you have feelings," she said. "But they don't run you."

"They might," Wyatt said. "If they was strong enough."

"Lord, God," she said. "That would be something to see."

"It would?"

"It would," Josie said. "Then you would really be dangerous."

Wyatt didn't comment. And they continued down Fremont Street, past the Harwood House toward Third Street, walking quietly, feeling no discomfort in their silence.

Twelve

Mattie had gone to bed already when Allie Earp came into Wyatt's front room without knocking.

"Virgil wants you up on Allen Street, Wyatt. Some cowboys are shooting at the moon, and Marshal White and Virgil have gone up there."

Wyatt took his Colt revolver from the top of the sideboard, looked to see that it was loaded, and headed out the door without saying anything. It was near the end of October and nights had grown cool in the desert. But the air was still, and Wyatt didn't mind being coatless. The moon was high and clear and nearly full as he hurried up Fremont Street, and then up Fourth to Allen. The street was full of people. One of the bartenders was standing outside Hafford's Saloon looking up toward the east end of Allen.

"Up there, Wyatt," he said. "Sixth Street."

Wyatt kept going. Several other men on the street recognized him and pointed east. From the corner of Sixth Street, Wyatt could see his brother and Fred White halfway down the block toward Toughnut Street, near where Morgan was rooming for a time with Fred Dodge. They were walking toward a group of cowboys. Wyatt walked after them. As Virgil and the city marshal approached, the group scattered, heading into the darkness among the cribs east of Sixth. One man stayed, facing Virgil and Fred White, a big man, hatless, with a lot of curly black hair. He had his pistol out. As Virgil and White approached the cowboy, Virgil separated away from White, stepping into the street and coming at the cowboy from his right, while White came at him straight on.

"Evening's over, Bill," White said, and put out his hand.

The cowboy moved the gun toward White, and Virgil came in from his right side and locked his arms around him.

White said, "Gimme the gun, Bill."

There was a single gunshot, and White staggered backward. Wyatt reached them as the shot sounded, and he slammed his big Colt against the side of the cowboy's head. The cowboy sagged, and his gun fell to the ground. White was down. The gunshot at close range had set his shirt on fire, and Morgan, who had rushed out of Fred Dodge's cabin at the sound of the shots, dropped to his knees to pat it out with his hands. When he was finished his hands were bloody.

"Fred's shot," he said.

Wyatt looked closely at the dazed cowboy that Virgil still held in a bear hug.

"Curley Bill," Wyatt said. "You sonova bitch."

"Gun went off," Curley Bill said.

"He ain't lying," Fred White said, lying quietly on the ground. "I could see he didn't pull the trigger."

Still kneeling beside White, Morgan picked up Curley Bill's gun and handed it up to Wyatt.

"Go get some help for Fred," Virgil said. "Can you stand by yourself, Bill?"

Curley Bill said he could, and Virgil let him go. Fred Dodge, who had come out of his cabin behind Morgan, started up the street on the run for Dr. Goodfellow.

"Five rounds still in the cylinder," Wyatt said to Virgil, looking at Curley Bill's gun.

He opened the cylinder and worked the hammer.

"Looks to me like he's got the trigger sear filed so he can fan it."

"No wonder it went off," Virgil said. "Where you shot, Fred?"

"Gut shot, Virgil."

None of the Earps said anything. They all knew the news was bad.

"Bill Brocius," Wyatt said. "I got to arrest you for shooting City Marshal Fred White."

"Virgil hadn't 'a grabbed me, it wouldn't 'a happened."

"Maybe," Wyatt said. "Still got to arrest you."

He put his hand on Curley Bill's arm. As he did so, gunfire came from one of the arroyos behind the cribs east of Sixth. Bullets thudded into the house behind them. All three Earps turned, and shot into the darkness. After the gunfire, the silence was intense. No more shots were fired from the arroyo.

"Go see if we hit something," Virgil said. And Morgan headed into the arroyo as Dr. Goodfellow rounded the corner at Allen Street and walked briskly toward them carrying his medical bag. His assistant followed, carrying a folded canvas stretcher. Morgan's voice came from the darkness.

"Nothing here, Virg."

Morgan came back from the arroyo, his pistol holstered. He had to push his way through the crowd that had gathered once the shooting stopped. Goodfellow arrived and dropped to his knees beside Fred White. The pool of blood under White had spread.

"Gut shot, Doc, down here."

Goodfellow unbuttoned White's pants and felt under White's shirt. He shook his head. The crowd was very quiet. The sound of Goodfellow's long inhale was loud in the silence.

"Not good, Fred."

"I know," White said.

A kind of audible sigh went through the crowd.

"I had five rounds left in my gun," Curley Bill said. "The sixth round went into the marshal. So how could I have been shooting up the street?"

"Maybe you didn't," Virgil said. "Or maybe you reloaded."

Someone in the crowd said, "The bastard admits he shot Fred."

The crowd moved in closer to the small group in the center.

"You and Morgan better take the prisoner to jail," Virgil said. "I'll be along soon as we see to Fred."

Wyatt nodded at Morgan and, one on each side, they walked Curley Bill through the crowd down Sixth to Toughnut Street where the jail stood on the corner. People moved out of the way sullenly, but no one impeded them. Several members of the crowd followed them silently to the jail and stood outside after they went in. Wyatt and Morgan both armed themselves with shotguns, but nothing came of the crowd, and by the time Virgil arrived it had dispersed.

Thirteen

It took Fred White two days to die calmly of peritonitis. Wyatt and Mattie walked alone back from the funeral in the early afternoon, on a bright fall day with no wind and the Dragoon Mountains clear and sharp against the cloudless sky northeast of Tombstone.

"They appointed a new city marshal?" Mattie said.

She rested her hand lightly on Wyatt's crooked arm as they walked.

"Virgil, sort of."

"Sort of?"

"Made him assistant marshal," Wyatt said, "but since there's no marshal he's actually the one."

"Why not just make him city marshal, then?"

Wyatt shrugged.

"Too many Rebs in the council," Wyatt said. "They needed someone quick, 'fore the cowboys moved in and rawhided the town, and Virgil's the man for the job. But the Rebs don't want to give it permanent to a Republican."

"So they sort of half did it," Mattie said.

"Just till the special election," Wyatt said.

"Won't Virgil have a head start, though?" Mattie said. "Being as he's already in the job?"

"Maybe."

They paused at the foot of Fremont Street and looked back at the cemetery on the top of the small rise where Fred White was.

"I'm glad you weren't hurt," Mattie said.

Wyatt nodded.

"Yes," he said. "I know you are."

"You don't seem much to care about me anymore," Mattie said. "But I care about you, Wyatt."

"I know."

"You don't," Mattie said, "do you?"

"Care about you?"

"Yes."

"You use my name. I support you. I don't embarrass you, running to the whores all the time."

"I know. You're good that way, Wyatt. You do your duty. But you don't love me, do you?"

Wyatt was silent for a while, looking across at Boot Hill and at the long empty sweep of hard country beyond it.

"No, I guess I don't," he said.

"Then why in hell did you take up with me, if you didn't love me?"

Again Wyatt was silent for a time, looking out at the barren land.

"God, Mattie, I don't know. I guess it was Jim had a woman and Virgil had a woman, and it was time for me to have a woman."

"And I was there," she said.

Wyatt nodded slowly.

"That's about the truth of it, Mattie."

Mattie's head dropped and her shoulders shook, but she made no sound.

"I'm sorry, Mattie, I really am."

She didn't look up or speak. She turned, with her head still down and her shoulders still shaking, and walked away from him, toward the front door of the house they shared. Wyatt watched her go. He wished he loved her. He wished he could even like her. But he didn't love her and he couldn't seem to like her. At best, he realized, all he could do was feel sorry.

"Goddamn," he said out loud.

But there was no one to hear him, and so he stood alone and silent in the still day, under the high blue sky, and looked at the door that Mattie had closed behind her, and thought of Josie Marcus.

Fourteen

Josie wasn't like any women he knew, Wyatt thought as he sat with her and Johnny Behan in their front room. She sat in on business. Allie was full of opinions on what Virgil ought to do. Even Mattie sometimes had suggestions and asked questions. But it was in private, at home, and when the business was to be decided the men went to a saloon and decided it. Josie acted like a man. As if business were as much hers as Behan's. He admired it in her, though he knew that if Mattie acted that way, he would be angry. He felt a small, sad amusement at his unfairness.

"You been thinking any on what we talked about, Wyatt?" Behan said.

"No."

"Well, damn it, Wyatt, I wish you would," Behan said. "If you resign as deputy, Charlie will appoint me, and I can show John Fremont that I've got experience as a lawman when they make the new county. I get to be sheriff. I make you under sheriff. I handle the civil part. You handle the criminal part, and we split the fees."

"Fremont's a Republican," Wyatt said. "Maybe

I should try for sheriff. Put my brothers on as deputies, keep all the fees."

"You can't get appointed. The governor may be Republican, but the county is all mostly Democrats," Behan said. "Ain't a cowboy alive going to sit still for having an Earp appointed sheriff."

When he was talking politics, Wyatt noticed, Behan's voice was much firmer.

"Johnny makes a good point," Josie said. "It's pretty certain you couldn't get the job, nor Virgil, nor Morgan."

"But Fremont would appoint for Johnny," Wyatt said.

"Yes. He's close to Fremont. He's quite close to the cowboys."

Behan was quiet, watching Josie and Wyatt. Johnny's not stupid, Wyatt thought. He knows she's making more progress than he is. Johnny was a vain man, but it was interesting to see that vanity didn't run him.

"Close to Curley Bill?"

"I got no problem with Brocius," Behan said.

"Got a problem with him killing Fred White?"

"He was acquitted of that," Josie said.

"Fred's dead," Wyatt said.

"Even Marshal White said it was an accident."

Wyatt knew he had said that, and maybe it was. But it wasn't an accident that Curley Bill had his gun out, and it wasn't an accident that he pointed it at Fred White. Wyatt was looking directly into Josie's eyes and she back at him, and he could feel them dissolve into each other like two streams merging. He held her look and felt almost as if they had coupled. He didn't say anything.

"It's no sin in politics," Josie said, after what seemed to Wyatt a long silence, "to be close to all sorts of people."

"Maybe there is no sin in politics," Wyatt said.

"If you feel that way," Josie said, "then you wouldn't want to try for sheriff anyway."

Her face was intense. Intelligence flickered in her eyes like heat lightning. Behan watched them closely. Could he feel it? Wyatt wondered. Johnny didn't miss a lot. Maybe Johnny felt it, and saw it and was trying to use it. Was she? No. She wasn't. He found that he was smiling.

"Maybe you should try, Josie," he said.

"If I thought I could win, I might," Josie said. "But I can't win, and neither can you, Wyatt. Johnny can win, and if he wins you win too. And I win. We all win. Besides, if I were sheriff, I'd have to smoke a smelly cigar and wear a big, ugly gun."

"That'd be a sight," Behan said.

All of them laughed.

"Do it, Wyatt," Josie said, "step aside. For Johnny, for yourself, for me. It's the right thing."

She was like a terrier after a rat, he thought. And very beautiful.

"Sure," Wyatt said. "I'll do it today."

"By God, Wyatt, that's the way," Behan said. "And you've got my word on the rest of it. I'll keep my part of the bargain."

"How about my brothers?" Wyatt said.

Behan didn't hesitate.

"Certainly," Behan said. "It's going to be a big county. There will be enough for everybody."

He put out his hand, and Wyatt, still looking at Josie, shook it briefly. Behan smiled with pleasure and thought about what he'd said, and liked it so much that he said it again.

"There will be enough for everybody. Everybody."

Behan was probably lying, Wyatt thought, still looking at Josie. Johnny didn't always mean what he said, and sometimes he didn't even know he didn't. But Wyatt didn't care. Wyatt knew why he had agreed to it. Later that day, he wrote a one-line letter of resignation: "I have the honor herewith to resign the office of deputy sheriff of Pima County."

Fifteen

Allie was cooking bacon and biscuits for all of them.

"How could anybody vote for Ben Sippy 'stead of you, Virgil?" she said.

Virgil drank some coffee, and put the cup down and wiped his mustache.

"Ben Sippy's a good man," he said.

"Not as good as you," she said.

Allie put a plate of biscuits on the table and began to fork thick slices of bacon out of the frying pan onto another platter. Virgil took a biscuit.

"Don't matter whether he's any good or not," Wyatt said. "Vote was three hundred eleven for Ben, two hundred nine for Virgil. It's done."

Allie put the bacon on the table.

"And Wyatt ain't deputy anymore, and Morgan plays pool more than he works."

Morgan took a piece of bacon in his fingers and ate it.

"And damn it, use a fork and knife at my table," Allie said.

Morgan grinned at her.

"You cook too good, Allie. I can't take the time."

She pretended to hit him with her big serving fork.

"So what are we going to do, Virgil?"

"Right now we're going to eat breakfast," Virgil said.

"I can see that," Allie said. "But I want to know what we're going to do for money."

"Make some more biscuits, Allie."

"You ain't finished them."

"But we will," Virgil said, "and then we'll want some more."

Virgil's voice didn't change, but Allie stopped talking and began to cut flour and lard together. She knew how far Virgil could be pushed. Which was farther by her than by anyone else. She wasn't afraid of his anger. She knew he wouldn't hurt her. But she loved him, and she didn't want to make him mad.

The men were quiet for a while, eating.

Then Morgan said, "So how come you resigned, Wyatt?"

Wyatt finished his coffee, and Allie brought the pot over from the stove and poured him some more. It was November and overcast. There was a wind coming off of the Dragoon Mountains to the east, and it drove a fine rattle of grit against the back windows of the kitchen.

"They're going to break up Pima County," Wyatt said. "Make a new county with Tombstone in the middle of it. Means there's going to be a lot of politics going on, and I kind of wanted to stop working for a Democrat before that happened."

"You think Bob Paul will make a run for sheriff?" Morgan asked.

"I think he will, and he's a Republican and we should be supporting him. Won't hurt us with John Clum either."

Virgil nodded.

"And that quarter interest in the Oriental is bringing in some profit," he said. "And the five hundred leasing our share of the Comstock mine to Emmanuel. And we got the north extension of the Mountain Maid claim."

Wyatt knew all of this, and so did Morgan. They knew that was for Allie's benefit. All three of them knew, also, that the share of the Oriental and the lease on the Comstock share were Wyatt's. But the brothers never distinguished ownership among themselves. And all three of them knew that. And so did Allie, who appeared to be totally absorbed in rolling out the biscuits.

"Still, you being deputy sheriff might have been helpful," Virgil said.

Wyatt said nothing.

"John Clum likes you," Virgil said. "Says he wants a two-gun man for sheriff. I know he's talking to Fremont about you."

"He can talk to Fremont whether I'm deputy sheriff or not," Wyatt said.

Virgil stirred sugar into his coffee, nodding his head slowly while he did it.

"True," he said.

They were quiet again. Allie brought the new batch of biscuits to the table. The men ate. Virgil looked at Wyatt thoughtfully.

But all he said was, "That new woman of Behan's is pretty good-looking."

"Can't say what she sees in Johnny," Morgan said.

"From San Francisco," Virgil said. "Heard her father's got money. Heard he bought that house for her and Behan."

"So what's she see in Behan?"

"No accounting for the man a woman'll take up with," Virgil said.

"Ain't that the truth," Allie said from the stove.

And Virgil reached over and gave her a slap on the backside. He and Morgan laughed, and Wyatt smiled a little and ate another biscuit.

Sixteen

It was early evening after dark. Wyatt was with Morgan in the Wells Fargo office. Wyatt, in from Bisbee, and Morgan, from Benson, were standing by with their shotguns while the strongbox was opened and the money locked in the safe.

Virgil came into the office with a boy, maybe nineteen. The boy looked frantic.

"Johnny-Behind-the-Deuce," Virgil said, nodding at the boy. "Shot a man in Charleston, they want to lynch him."

The Wells Fargo clerk swung the door shut on the big black safe and straightened up.

"You can't keep him here," the clerk said.

None of the three brothers looked at him.

"Who'd he shoot?" Wyatt said.

"Mining engineer named Schneider."

"Hell, I know him," Morgan said. "He manages the smelter over in San Pedro."

"Well, now he don't," Virgil said.

"You gotta hide me," Johnny-Behind-the-Deuce said. "They're gonna kill me." His eyes were damp as if he had been crying, and his voice sounded thick.

"No," Virgil said. "They ain't going to kill you."

"You got to get him out of this office," the clerk said.

"We'll take him across to Vronan's," Virgil said. "Jim's there. Morgan, you go down and tell Ben Sippy where we are. Have him bring Behan and anybody else he can get, and meet us there. Tell them to bring a buggy."

"You see Doc," Wyatt said, "bring him along."

Morgan nodded. He gave Virgil his shotgun and left, running.

"We don't need Doc," Virgil said.

"Good gun," Wyatt said.

Johnny-Behind-the-Deuce was crying again.

"They're gonna find me," he sobbed. "We can't stay here. They're gonna find me."

Without looking at him, Virgil patted Johnny-Behind-the-Deuce on the shoulder.

"Get him outta here now," the Wells Fargo clerk said. "I don't want to have to report you to the regional manager."

"He's a good gun," Virgil said. "But he's crazy."

"That's right, and it scares hell out of the kind of citizens who might want to string up Johnny-Behind-the-Deuce."

"You got a point," Virgil said. "C'mon."

He put an arm around Johnny-Behind-the-Deuce and turned him toward the door.

"I ain't going out first," Johnny-Behind-the-Deuce said.

Tears were running down his face.

"Wyatt'll go first," Virgil said.

"You crying when you jerked on Schneider?" Wyatt said.

Johnny-Behind-the-Deuce cried harder. Wyatt shook his head and went out the front door onto Allen Street with his shotgun. His left arm around Johnny-Behind-the-Deuce, and Morgan's shotgun in his right hand, Virgil followed him. Up Allen Street at the east end of town, a group of miners was gathered. Both Wyatt and Virgil walked with the shotguns by their side, muzzle down and aiming at the ground. The miners saw them. A guttural mass murmur came from the miners, and one voice above the rest said, "There he is."

Virgil and Wyatt kept walking across Allen. Johnny-Behind-the-Deuce would have run, but Virgil's grip on his shoulders kept him in check.

"Walk easy," Virgil said.

"Like dogs," Wyatt said to Johnny-Behind-the-Deuce. "You run, they'll chase you."

Johnny-Behind-the-Deuce continued to sob. He was much shorter than Virgil and slight. And he was shaking with fear.

"Where'd you get him?" Wyatt said.

"Constable from Charleston, tall skinny fella, big Adam's apple, I can't remember his name, was trying to get him out of town ahead of the mob. I was out on the Charles-town Road running the stallion, and the constable recognizes me and says, 'You got a fast horse, you take him into Tombstone.' So I put him up behind me, and here we come."

"That stallion'll run away from anything in Arizona," Wyatt said. "'Less, a 'course, he stops to kill it."

"Just got to step careful when you come up on him," Virgil said.

The mob was beginning to move down the street toward them when they reached Vronan's. There were several townspeople bowling, and the bar was crowded.

"Might be a fight here pretty quick," Virgil said loudly. "You don't want to be in it, you might head out now."

Behind the bar, Jim Earp said, "Don't worry about the tabs, drinks on the house."

The building emptied at once.

"Vronan going to like that?" Wyatt said.

"No," James said.

Wyatt went to the front door and stood leaning on the left jamb, looking up the street, the shotgun hanging against his right leg. James took a big Navy Colt from under the bar. He held it in his left hand in a way that said he was right-handed.

"Can't do much at a distance anymore," he said to Virgil. "But up close I can still do damage."

"Got a lynch mob after this child," Virgil said. "Ben Sippy's on the way with Morgan and some others. Got a back door?"

"Yes, but Vronan keeps it locked, don't want anybody sneaking in and rolling a couple of strings."

"Okay. Sit with Johnny-Behind-the-Deuce. I'll go out front with Wyatt and wait for Morgan."

Johnny-Behind-the-Deuce was sniffling. He had come to view Virgil as his only safety.

"I want to go with you," he said.

"No you don't," Virgil said. "I'm going out and stare down the miners."

"Your brother can do that."

"Probably can," Virgil said. "But I'm going to help him."

Johnny-Behind-the-Deuce started to cry again.

"This here is my brother, James," Virgil said. "You stay with him."

The miners were gathered in the street outside the bowling alley. Behind them, across the street, was a larger group of townspeople watching. Virgil stood on the other side of the doorway from Wyatt and leaned his back on the wall with the butt of the shotgun resting on his hip, the barrels pointing toward the sky. Both men looked straight at the miners.

One of the miners said, "We want the murderous little bastard, Virgil."

He was a squat man, with a sparse beard.

Virgil shook his head.

"You better give him to us, Virgil, or we'll, by God, take him."

Virgil shook his head again, and Wyatt brought the shotgun up and aimed it quite carefully at the miner.

"I'll shoot him, Virgil," Wyatt said. "Who you going to kill?"

Virgil scanned the miners slowly without answering.

From the back of the mob someone yelled, "You can't kill us all."

Virgil let the muzzle of the shotgun drop so that it leveled at the miners.

"Might," Virgil said.

"How many people you think you can hit?" Wyatt said, staring at the group of miners. His voice was loud enough to be heard across the street. "You let fly both barrels at this distance?"

"Always wondered," Virgil said.

The miners were silent for a moment. They knew who the Earps were. Several of the men had rifles. But the mob was different from the men who made it up. The mob was edgy and full of repressed movement.

"We ain't going to let him go, Virgil."

It was the squat miner again. Virgil said nothing. He cocked both hammers on the shotgun. The sound crackled through the tension.

"This the day you want to die?" Wyatt said.

Without looking, Wyatt could feel his brother James in the doorway. James couldn't shoot much since he got crippled up in the war. But he had the big Navy Colt, and at this range he could do damage.

Ben Sippy, the city marshal, rounded the corner at Fifth Street with Johnny Behan, the deputy sheriff. Both of them had Winchesters. Both of them were on foot. Behind them was a group of deputized saloon men on horseback. Driving a light spring wagon was Morgan. His revolver was on the seat beside him.

"All right, you men," Sippy shouted, "clear the street."

Morgan drove the wagon directly at the gathered miners, who gave way as the two-horse team passed through. The deputies fanned out across Allen Street on their horses directly between the miners and Vronan's.

"Why'nt you bring the prisoner out, Virgil," Sippy said as he reached the doorway where the Earps were standing.

Still looking straight at the miners, now partly shielded by the horsemen, Virgil leaned his head back in through the doorway and said, "Send him on out, James."

James Earp half pushed, half led Johnny-Behind-the-Deuce out of Vronan's bowling alley.

"Get in the wagon, son," Sippy said.

Johnny-Behind-the-Deuce looked at Virgil, his eyes red and swollen. Virgil nodded and jerked his head at the wagon. Johnny-Behind-the-Deuce hung back.

"Get up there, boy," Virgil said, "beside my brother."

Morgan picked up his revolver and stuck it into his belt,

and Johnny-Behind-the-Deuce climbed up on the wagon and sat beside him. Standing in front of the mounted deputies, Sippy spoke to the miners.

"Deputy Morgan Earp and the other deputies are going to take this boy down to Benson and get on a train with him and take him to Tucson, where he will be tried for the murder of W. P. Schneider."

"Save a lot of trouble, Ben, we just hang him here," the squat miner said in a conversational tone.

"Trouble ain't the issue," Sippy said. "I want all you men to go back to whatever you was doing before you almost made a bunch of damn fools out of yourselves."

"Hell, Ben," one of the miners shouted, "I was up at Nosey Kate Lowe's."

"Well, we know what you was doing, don't we?" Sippy answered, and the miners laughed.

Morgan clucked at the team, and the wagon began to move. With the deputized gunmen riding on either side of it, the wagon picked up speed as it went down Allen Street. It turned right at Fourth Street and disappeared. Many of the miners watched it and then when it was gone began to drift away from in front of Vronan's. The onlookers went back into the saloons, and after a time the street was empty. Virgil eased the hammers down on the shotgun and looked at his brother. Wyatt was still staring after the last miner, the shotgun still leveled.

"Well, that's over," Virgil said.

Wyatt looked startled, then he took a deep breath and let it out and slowly lowered the shotgun. He eased the hammers off cock. James spoke from the doorway.

"Vronan can afford a couple more on the house, I figure."

"Whiskey sounds right," Virgil said.

James said, "You want coffee, Wyatt?"

"Coffee'd be good."

And the three brothers went in and stood together at the dimly lit bar in the empty bowling alley and drank and didn't say much.

CHRONICLE

In New York City, James Garfield is shot and badly wounded by Charles Guiteau. The President dies of his wounds in September . . . In New Mexico, William Bonney is shot to death by Pat Garrett . . . In Canada, Sitting Bull surrenders . . . The Boston Symphony Orchestra performs its first concert . . . In Germany the first electric tramway begins operations . . . in Boston Walt Whitman's publisher withdraws "Leaves of Grass," after widespread charges that the poem is indecent.

* * *

PARNELL PROMISES IRELAND HELP FROM AMERICA
Dublin, October 25—
Mr. Parnell and Mr. O'Connor were entertained at a banquet in Galway today. Mr. Parnell, in speaking, said if Irishmen would call upon their brothers in America for help and would show they had a fair chance for success they would have America's trained and organized assistance in breaking the yoke now encircling them.

* * *

AN OPEN REVOLT AGAINST THE WHITES AT NATAL

The Most Horrible Atrocities Committed by the Natives.

London, October 26—

Later advices from Cape Town confirm the alarming news received yesterday, announcing that other tribes have joined the Basutos in open revolt against the colonial government. The natives beyond Pieter Maritsberg, the capital of Natal, situated fifty miles from Port Natal, have made an attack on the white residents and such natives as remain faithful to the Cape government, burning buildings, pillaging, and outraging women. The most horrible atrocities are reported, and the insurgents are complete masters of the situation. The colonial authorities are in need of immediate assistance, and unless reinforcements can reach them at once, the situation of the little handful of men commanded by Colonel Clark is considered absolutely hopeless. A later dispatch sent by the Union Steamships Company's Durban agent states that all communication between Durban and the Cape colony has been cut off, the Basutos having cut the wire.

* * *

LYDIA E. PINKHAM'S VEGETABLE COMPOUND

A Positive Cure

For All Female Complaints

This preparation, as the name signifies, consists of vegetable properties that are harmless to the most delicate invalid . . . it will cure entirely the worst form of Falling of the Uterus, Leucorrhoea, Irregular and Painful menstruation, all Ovarian Troubles, Inflammation and Ulceration, Floodings, all Displacements and the consequent spinal weakness, and is especially adapted to the Change of Life. It will dissolve and expel tumors from the uterus in an early stage of development. The tendency to Cancerous Humors there is checked very speedily by its use.

In fact, it has proved to be the greatest and best remedy that has ever been discovered. It permeates every portion of the system, and gives new life and vigor. It removes faintness, flatulency, destroys all craving for stimulants, and relieves weakness of the stomach.

It cures Bloating, Headaches, Nervous Prostration, General Debility, Sleeplessness, Depression and Indigestion. That feeling of bearing down, causing pain, weight and backache, is permanently cured by its use. It will at all times and under all circumstances, act in harmony with the law that governs the female system.

For kidney complaints of either sex this compound is unsurpassed.

* * *

EPPS COCOA

By a thorough knowledge of the natural laws which govern the operations of digestion and nutrition, and by careful application of the fine properties of well-selected Cocoa, Mr. Epps has provided our breakfast tables with a delicately flavored beverage which may save us many heavy doctors bills . . .

James Epps & Co.

London, Eng.

Seventeen

It was early March. Wyatt was dealing faro in the Oriental and drinking coffee and watching the room. He wasn't looking for John Tyler. John Tyler had never come back into the Oriental, and Wyatt heard he had moved on. Wyatt was just watching the room, as he watched every room he was ever in. He looked at everything around him and had for as long as he could remember. He could see farther than most men, and even as a child he was aware of what was happening behind him, as much as he was of what went on in front. He saw Josie Marcus the moment she came into the saloon.

She stood a moment, until her eyes adjusted, then she looked around the room and saw Wyatt and smiled and started over.

"Game's closed, gentlemen," Wyatt said.

He paid off the winners, collected from the losers and was on his feet by the time Josie reached him. She had on a very pleasant cologne.

"Here you are," Josie said.

The room was half full in the afternoon, and lively. The noise didn't abate, but a lot of the men and all of the whores paused to look at Josie Marcus.

"Hello, Josie."

"I didn't mean to interrupt your game."

"You can interrupt anytime," he said. "Don't see anyone like you in here very often."

"A lady?" she said. "Like me?"

"Yes, ma'am."

"Oh hell, Wyatt, I used to work in places like this."

"I thought your daddy had money."

"He does."

Josie sat in one of the chairs vacated when the card game closed.

"So how come you were working in saloons?"

"May I have a drink?" Josie said.

Wyatt looked at her silently for a moment, then signaled to one of the bartenders.

"I'd like some whiskey," Josie said when the bartender came over. "With water."

The bartender looked at her, and then at Wyatt. Wyatt nodded, and the bartender went and got it.

"Am I shocking you?" Josie said to Wyatt after the bartender had left.

"You're interesting me," Wyatt said. "How come you worked in saloons?"

"Same reason I was an actress," she said.

"Which was?"

"I thought it might be fun," she said.

"And?"

"And it was for a little while."

"Then Behan came along?" Wyatt said.

"Yes. And I thought he might be fun."

"And?"

"And," Josie said, "he was for a little while."

She looked straight into his face when she said it. And had a swallow of whiskey and drank some water behind it. Wyatt sipped his coffee, holding the cup in both hands, looking at her over the cup. Then he smiled. She had never seen him smile. Though he was always polite, he was always reserved, and the smile was startling. When he smiled, all of him smiled. His mouth, his eyes, his whole face. He was so of a piece, she thought, that his whole person seemed to express him.

"Now you've come along," Josie said.

"You think I might be fun?" Wyatt said.

"I think you might be a lot of fun," Josie said.

They looked at each other in silence. Josie drank a little more whiskey. She knew who he was. She knew he was dangerous. She could see what Clay Allison had seen. What is it? She had thought about it since she'd met him. He was different from other men she had known. Different from Behan. Maybe it wasn't something. Maybe what she was seeing was the absence of something, like looking at the dark.

"Behan's up to Tucson till Thursday," Josie said. "Now that he's the new sheriff, he's up there a lot."

"Johnny always liked the political stuff," Wyatt said.

Josie kept studying Wyatt's face.

"I hate to eat alone," she said.

Wyatt drank the rest of his coffee and put the cup down slowly. She loved how precise he was. How even his smallest gesture seemed perfectly controlled.

"I'd be pleased to buy you dinner at the Russ House," Wyatt said.

"I accept," she said. "But first I'd like another whiskey."

Wyatt nodded at the bartender, and he brought her another drink. Wyatt had more coffee. The only effect the whiskey seemed to have on her was to heighten the color in her cheeks. Her big dark eyes remained clear and challenging. Her speech still sounded what he always assumed to be upper class. She met the glances of people in the Oriental straight on. She drank the whiskey, Wyatt thought, without pretense. She didn't act like it was too strong, the way many women did when given whiskey. She didn't sip it like tea, and she didn't gulp it like a drunken miner. She took a swallow, chased it with water. She wasn't thinking about it. And it didn't appear to be anything she needed. It was just something she chose to do while talking with him. Her clothes were good. He couldn't tell why, but he knew they were. Too good for Behan's income. Her father, probably. Like the house. Behan's luck had been good.

They ate chicken fricassee at the Russ House and afterward they walked through the town. The March evening had not yet settled, but the sun was gone and there was a bluish cast to the light.

"I like Tombstone at this time of day," Josie said. "It looks nicer than it is."

"I like it early in the morning," Wyatt said. "Before people are on the street."

Josie laughed.

"I've never seen it then," she said.

"Not an early bird?"

"No," she said, "a night owl."

They walked up Fifth Street, past the Vizina mine. The streets were busy.

"Johnny never wants me to walk around town. Not even with him. Says it's undignified."

"Probably is," Wyatt said.

"Probably," Josie said.

Past the Palace Lodging House across the street, an alley ran up to Sixth Street.

"Curley Bill killed Fred White down there," Wyatt said. "Other end of the alley."

"I heard he was acquitted," Josie said.

"Fred said it was an accident, 'fore he died."

"Wasn't it just about cowboys being noisy on the street?"

"Yes."

At Allen Street they stopped by Meyers clothing store. Across the street the Crystal Palace stood on one corner and the Oriental on the other.

"Luke Short killed Charlie Storms right there last month," Wyatt said.

"Why?"

"Charlie was drunk," Wyatt said. "Pushed Luke into it."

"Did you know them?"

"Sure," Wyatt said. "Knew Luke back in Dodge."

"Is he a good fighting man?"

"You don't want to jerk on Luke Short," Wyatt said.

"Would you?"

Wyatt smiled.

"I'd get my brothers," Wyatt said. "Outnumber him."

"But you're not afraid of him, are you?"

Wyatt looked startled.

"No," he said. "'Course not."

Josie smiled to herself.

"People die for so little in Tombstone," she said.

"Not just Tombstone," Wyatt said.

They stood quietly on the corner for a time watching the miners and cowboys moving in and out of the saloons. Light and sound splashed into the street when the saloon doors opened. There were saddle horses in the street, but very little wheeled traffic.

"We got some mining interests," Wyatt said. "Office is down there, this side of the Grand."

Josie nodded, but he could see she wasn't interested in mining.

"What's up this way?" she said, looking to her right.

"Past Sixth Street is whorehouses," Wyatt said.

"Let's walk up there."

"It's kind of raw," he said.

"Oh good," she said.

He smiled, and they turned right on Allen Street past the retail stores, mostly closed for the night, and the Arizona Brewery, still open. A construction site stood near the corner of Sixth, with a building half completed.

"Going to be the Bird Cage Theatre," Wyatt said. "Bill Hutchinson's putting it up."

"Not a saloon," she said.

"Well, a saloon too," Wyatt said.

"I swear if they put up a convent," Josie said, "it would have a saloon in the front."

And they both laughed as they crossed the street into the bordello district.

No one paid much attention to Josie east of Sixth Street. They assumed she was a whore. But several people glanced at Wyatt.

"People are surprised to see you here," Josie said.

"Haven't spent much time here."

"Faithful to what's-her-name?"

"Mattie. I didn't think I should embarrass her."

"And now?"

"Now I'm with you," he said.

By the time they walked back along Fremont Street it was dark. They turned up Third Street and stood for a moment on the front porch of her house. During the entire afternoon and evening they had not touched each other. They did not touch now.

"I'm not going to ask you in," Josie said.

"All right," Wyatt said.

"I will someday, I think. But now is too soon."

"I have time," Wyatt said.

"But I would like you to kiss me good night," she said.

"That would be fine," Wyatt said.

Eighteen

Bat Masterson walked into the Oriental with his bedroll across one shoulder, wearing two Colt revolvers and carrying a Sharps rifle, and sat down in a chair at Wyatt's table. A big, high-shouldered horse wrangler named Bear shook his head at him.

"Don't want no new players this game," he said. "Break the way the cards are falling."

Masterson paid no attention.

"Wyatt," he said.

"Bat," Wyatt said.

"You hear me, boy?" Bear said.

Bat glanced at him curiously for a moment and turned back toward Wyatt.

"Hear they might be hiring here," he said.

Wyatt nodded and started to deal.

"Don't you deal with him at the table," Bear said.

"Friend of mine," Wyatt said. "I'll deal around him."

"Don't care if he's a friend of the Virgin Mary," Bear said. "I don't want my luck changed."

Wyatt looked almost as if he was going to smile.

"You going to change his luck, Bat?" Wyatt said.

Bat turned and looked at Bear. He was half Bear's size. His eyes were a very pale blue.

"You want me to change your luck, cowboy?" Bat said.

Bear's mouth opened and closed. He tried to hold Bat's look and couldn't.

Finally he said, "Aw shit," and folded his hand.

No one else spoke.

"I'm out," he said.

He picked up his chips and walked away from the table. Wyatt gestured to the other players, and they handed in their cards.

"You in?" he said to Bat.

"Sure," he said.

Wyatt reshuffled and dealt again. By late afternoon, Bat had won four dollars, and Wyatt closed the game and took a table near the bar with Bat. Bat had a glass of whiskey. Wyatt had coffee.

"You really looking for work?" Wyatt said.

"Sure. Heard there was work here."

"We can use you," Wyatt said.

"I assume that some of the customers are tougher than Bear."

"Some."

"But not tougher than you and me," Bat said.

"Not yet," Wyatt said.

"Heard you and Virgil and Morg had a little standoff with a lynch mob."

"Mob's like a cattle herd," Wyatt said, "you know that. All you got to do is turn 'em. What you been doing?"

"Up in Ogallala," Bat said, "with Ben Thompson."

"Peace officering?"

Bat laughed.

"Not exactly," he said. "Ben's brother Billy got himself in trouble up there. Me and Ben had to go up there and get him out 'fore they hung him."

"Woman?"

"'Course," Bat said. "Little whiskey mixed in. You know Billy."

"Meanest loudmouthed drunken little bastard I ever ran into," Wyatt said.

"Got Ben into a lot more trouble Ben ever got into himself," Bat said.

Wyatt shrugged.

"Blood's blood," he said. "You on the run?"

"No, we got him out clean. I left him and Ben in Dodge, got a train to Trinidad, hopped a Santa Fe work train far as it went and caught the stage over to Deming."

"Apache Country," Wyatt said.

"Yeah, they let me ride shotgun."

"Where they can get a clean shot at you," Wyatt said.

Masterson laughed.

"What was that story Lincoln told, 'Wasn't for the honor I'd just as soon walk'? Anyway, we got to Deming and I got a train to Benson, and took the stage in."

"Doc in town?" Masterson said.

Wyatt nodded.

"Big-Nose Kate is here with him," he said.

"For how long?"

Wyatt shrugged.

"Half an hour be a long time with Kate," he said.

Nineteen

Johnny's losing his hair, Wyatt thought as he sat across from Behan at a table near the back wall of the Oriental.

"The reason I wanted to talk with you, Wyatt, is this," Behan said.

He had a glass of beer in front of him. He put his hat down on the seat of an unused chair beside them. It was broad-brimmed like the cowboys wore. Most townsmen wore a shorter brim.

"You know," Behan said, "that there's a lot of conflict between the townspeople and the cowboys."

Wyatt didn't comment. He picked up his coffee cup in both hands and drank and held the cup in front of him as he listened.

"Lotta folks think cowboy is another word for rustler," Behan said. "And I know there's some rustling going on, but I figure it's mostly Mexican stock and . . ." He shrugged.

Wyatt waited.

"They'd be a good source of tax revenue if you could collect from them. They come into town regularly, and spend money here. What

I'm trying to do is, I'm trying to get to know the cowboys a little better, maybe smooth things out."

Wyatt drank some more coffee. Behan looked at him expectantly. Wyatt didn't say anything.

"God, you ain't a talkative man, are you," Behan said.

"No," Wyatt said. "I'm not."

"Well, you know all these cowboys, don't you?" Behan said.

"Yes."

"What can you tell me about them?"

"They're kind of rambunctious," Wyatt said.

"I know that," Behan said. "I was thinking we could talk some, you know. You tell me about the ones you know, and maybe I can get to know them; being on friendly terms, I might be able to keep them from being so rambunctious."

"Fred White was on friendly terms," Wyatt said.

"Coroner's inquest held that to be an accidental shooting, Wyatt. You know that."

"Sure," Wyatt said.

Behan turned the beer glass slowly on the tabletop in front of him. The bubbles rose briskly through the beer. Earp always made him feel uncomfortable. Johnny thought of himself as a politician. He thought of the sheriff's job as a political job. Before he said something, he tried to figure out how other people would react to what he said. He tried not to offend. He tried to accommodate. Politics was compromise. Life was compromise. The way you succeeded was figuring people out, and using what you'd figured, to get them on your side. Johnny couldn't figure Earp out. He seemed disinterested in what other people thought. He showed no interest in compromise. He just went in a straight line toward wherever he was going and didn't pay much attention to what other people said. Johnny felt almost wistful for a moment. What would that be like?

"So tell me about Curley Bill," Behan said.

"Brocius? He's a pretty likable fella," Wyatt said. "Word's good. Polite around women. Laughs a lot. He wasn't a damn rustler, he might amount to something. Except when he's got a problem, the first thing he does is shoot at it."

"He looks pretty dangerous."

"Got a cute spin move with a gun," Wyatt said. "Offers it to you dangling on his finger, butt first, like he's going to surrender, you know, then spins it on the trigger guard and plonks you in the chest. You ever ask for his gun, have him drop it on the ground."

Behan nodded.

"I was a sheriff in Prescott, you know," he said.

"Fred White done some police work too," Wyatt said.

Behan nodded again.

"You sound like you like Brocius," Behan said.

"I do, but I ain't confused about him."

"How about John Ringo?" Behan said.

"He don't talk much either," Wyatt said.

"But he's dangerous," Behan said.

"Yes."

"Dangerous as Curley Bill?"

"More."

Behan stared thoughtfully into his beer glass for a moment. Then he lifted his head and leaned back a bit in his chair. Wyatt noticed that Behan hadn't drunk any of the beer. A careful man, Wyatt thought.

"Dangerous as your friend Holliday?" Behan said.

"Never been put to the test," Wyatt said.

"More dangerous than you?" Behan asked, and smiled as if to apologize for so brazen a question.

"Same answer," Wyatt said.

"Explain to me about you and Holliday," Behan said.

"I like him," Wyatt said.

Behan waited. Wyatt didn't say anything else.

Finally Behan said, "That's it?"

"Yes."

Behan thought about pushing the issue and decided not to. He had plenty of time to learn about Doc Holliday.

"What do you know about the rustling?" Behan said.

"Same thing everyone knows," Wyatt said. "It's back and forth across the border. Steal horses in Arizona, sell them in Mexico. Steal cattle in Mexico, sell them in Arizona."

"Ringo and Brocius are involved?"

"Yes."

"They have a headquarters?"

"Hear they got a camp in the Mountains."

"Chiricahuas?"

"Yes."

"You know where?"

"No."

"Could you find it?"

"Sure."

"But you have no reason to," Behan said.

"I deal cards," Wyatt said. "I'm in business with my brothers."

"Of course," Behan said. "Who else is involved?"

The bubbles had stopped rising in Behan's beer glass.

"The McLaury brothers got some holding pens down on the White River," Wyatt said. "Ike Clanton's got some pens at his place."

"They steal 'em or just receive 'em?" Behan said.

"McLaurys mostly receive. Clanton does both. Hell, Ike raids down in Sonora, steals two thousand cattle at a time."

"McLaurys dangerous?" Behan said.

"We're a fair piece down the danger scale from Ringo and Brocius," Wyatt said.

"Tell me about them."

"McLaurys and Clantons?"

Behan nodded.

"Well, Tom McLaury's all right, I guess. Quiet. Works hard. Probably works harder than he should, 'cause Frank don't work hardly at all. Frank's a strutter. Talks a lot.

Don't do much. Think's he's a ladies' man. Ike Clanton's a blowhard."

"How about his brother?"

"Billy?" Wyatt shrugged. "Billy's a dumb kid. Does what Ike tells him."

"Think I can get along with them?" Behan said.

"Seems like you can get along with anybody, Johnny."

"If I can get them smoothed down, it will be good for everybody, don't you think?"

"Sure."

"You think it can be done?" Behan said.

"If it serves them it can," Wyatt said. "Those boys mostly do what serves them."

"Anything you can do to help?" Behan said. "Your name means something."

"Might mean something to Ringo," Wyatt said, "or Curley Bill. McLaurys and the Clantons don't think much of us, ever since we caught 'em stealing mules from the Army."

"Nobody ever proved that," Behan said.

Wyatt smiled.

"So can you talk to any of them?" Behan said. "Ringo? Curley Bill?"

"That's lawman work," Wyatt said. "I'm in business with my brothers."

"Well, at least," Behan said, "I can count on you if there's trouble."

"Depends on the trouble," Wyatt said.

"Well, of course," Behan said. "'Course it would, Wyatt. And thanks for your help. Nice of you to give me your time."

Wyatt didn't say anything. Behan stood.

"Good to talk with you," Behan said.

Wyatt nodded, and Behan nodded back and stood for a moment and then turned and left. Wyatt sat without moving, holding his coffee, looking over the rim of the cup after Behan.

Twenty

The way Bob Paul told it later, to Wyatt riding beside him, after he had joined the posse, was that Bud Philpot had wanted Paul, who was the shotgun messenger, to drive the Benson stage that night.

"His bowels was all cramped up," Paul said. "So when we got to Contention, I give him the shotgun and took the reins. We was coming up out of a wash couple miles north of Contention, when a fella steps out and yells, 'Hold.' And then there's some other boys in the road and they're shooting and poor Bud gets it right through the gizzard."

"Wanted to eliminate the shooter right off," Wyatt said.

"Yep, so I grab the shotgun from Bud and get off both barrels with my right hand, hanging on to the reins and Bud with my left, and the team bolts, and one of the passengers, riding back in the dickey seat, says he's hit, and we're rolling like hell flat out now along the road with the team out of control, with the coach swaying, and I lose Bud off the side, and making a grab for him, I lose the reins and finally got to get down onto the wagon tongue to get them back and get the damned horses steadied. And I figure Bud's done anyway, and maybe I can save the passenger, fella named Roerig, so I keep her rolling on into Benson."

"Boys from Drews Station heard the shots," Wyatt said, "and then you went whooping on past. So they run out and found Bud and one of them come galloping into Tombstone yelling for the sheriff."

The first thing Behan had done when he got the report was to come into the Oriental looking for Wyatt.

"Benson stage was held up, Bud Philpot's dead, and we're organizing a sheriff's posse," Behan said.

"I'll get my brothers," Wyatt said.

They rode north from Tombstone just after sunrise. Three Earps, Bat Masterson, Doc Holliday, Marshall Williams, the Wells Fargo agent, Johnny Behan, and half a dozen of Behan's deputies. They picked up a trail where Philpot had died, and Billy Breakenridge, one of Behan's deputies and the best tracker in the posse, followed it across the shale-littered desert floor, the horses picking their way among the jagged desert plants. In patches where the desert earth was clear, Breakenridge would get off his horse and study the ground.

"Four riders, I think," Breakenridge said, squatting on his heels, his head bent. "Looks to me like we keep going the way they're going, we'll run right into Len Redfield's place."

"Cowboys," Doc Holliday said.

"Now, Doc," Behan said. "Don't go deciding things 'fore you know."

In an hour and a half, with the sun well above the horizon, they were sitting their horses in front of the small frame house that was the main building of the Redfield ranch. There was a stable past the house and an outhouse that looked as if it hadn't wintered well. Nobody came out of the house.

Virgil said, "See what's in the stable," and Morgan turned his horse with his knee and walked on down and into the open stable door. In a moment he rode back out and up to the group.

" 'Bout six horse," Morgan said. "Two of 'em been ridden hard and not long ago. They're still lathered."

Virgil nodded and squinted at the house.

He said to Behan, "Don't you think you ought to spread 'em out a little, Johnny?"

Behan nodded and gestured with his right hand, and the riders moved away from each other, putting space between them until they were in a half-circle in front of the silent house.

"Goddamned fool had us bunched up like quail," Doc said to Bat Masterson. Masterson shrugged.

Wyatt held his Winchester vertically in front of him, its butt resting against his saddle horn. Most of the men had Winchesters; Doc had a shotgun.

"Redfield," Behan shouted. "Len Redfield."

There was no sound but the ones the horses made: the snort of their breath, the sound of their hooves as they shifted patiently, the creak of leather, the small clink of the bits and buckles.

"You in the house," Behan said loudly, "you either come on out or we're coming in."

After a moment a tall man with narrow shoulders and a big belly stepped out onto the small front porch. He had on pants that had been washed threadbare, and colorless. He wore the suspenders over his undershirt.

"What you boys want?" he said.

"Benson stage got held up," Behan said. "Bud Philpot got killed. We tracked 'em here."

"I got nothing to do with no stage holdup," Redfield said.

"Got two horses in the barn," Behan said. "Been rode hard, and recent."

Virgil said, "Why don't we just take a look, John?"

Behan nodded.

"Go ahead," he said.

Wyatt's horse pricked his ears up and forward. Wyatt heard it too, behind the house. He moved the horse forward and around the corner of the house. Bent low as if to conceal himself, a man was running for the brush cover, trying to keep the house between him and the posse. Wyatt's horse shifted into a trot, and Wyatt caught up with the man and passed him and turned the horse in front of him.

Morgan came around the other side of the house on the dapple gray mare he was so proud of. As the man broke the other way, Wyatt turned him again and, with Morgan on the other side, slowly herded him, his desperate dashes becoming shorter and more breathless, back out in front of the house until he stood exhausted in front of the posse.

"You know him?" Behan said.

Redfield didn't speak.

"What's your name?" Behan said.

The man's breath was rasping loudly in and out. Behan had to ask him again.

"Luther . . ." he said. ". . . King."

"I'm Sheriff Behan," Johnny said. "I'm head of this posse, and we're looking for the people held up the Benson stage."

"I . . . didn't . . . have . . . nothing . . . to do . . . with that," King gasped.

"What you doing, sneaking out the back way?"

"I didn't do nothing but hold the horses," King said. "That's all. Just holding the horses. I didn't know there'd be no shooting."

Redfield stood motionless on his porch, his arms folded tight over his chest. The horsemen sat quietly in a semicircle around King so that he had to look up to look at them. Behan sat his big white-stockinged bay gelding directly in front of King.

"Who'd you hold the horses for?" Behan said.

"I can't tell you that," King said. "You know I can't peach on my friends like that."

Bob Paul leaned forward in his saddle, his forearms resting on the pommel.

"You know who this man is, Luther?" He nodded toward Holliday.

King shook his head.

"This is Doc Holliday. You know who Doc Holliday is, Luther?"

"Yes."

Holliday sat motionless on his horse and stared at King.

"You wonder why Doc Holliday is on a posse, him not being too much of a lawman usually?"

Behan smiled. Several of the riders laughed audibly. King shook his head.

"He's here on a mission of vengeance," Paul said. "His beloved Katy was on that stage, and somebody shot her."

"I didn't do no shooting," King said. "I just held the horses."

He looked down, and away from Holliday.

"Then you better tell me who done the shooting," Holliday said. His voice was hoarse and there was no inflection to it.

"I can't," King said.

Holliday lowered the shotgun slowly toward him.

"Somebody's going to die for Kate," Holliday rasped.

"For God's sake, man," Virgil said. "For your own sake, tell him."

"Who?" Holliday said.

Tears began to well in King's eyes.

"Billy Leonard," King blurted, his voice thick. "And Harry Head and Jim Crane. I just held the horses. I didn't see nothing. I didn't do nothing."

"Rustlers," Wyatt said.

"Where are they now?" Holliday rasped.

"They lit out. Head disappeared soon as the shooting started. Billy and Jim, they changed horses here, rode west across the river, going like hell."

"Lenny rides with the rustlers too," Wyatt said. "Him and his brother."

"Got nothing on Len," Behan said. "He had no way of knowing. He just traded some horses."

"And tried to let Luther here get away," Wyatt said.

"Appreciate your help on this, Wyatt, but I'm the sheriff, and you're just along to help shoot, you know what I mean."

Wyatt looked at Virgil, and both men smiled in a way that Behan didn't understand, though he knew he didn't like it.

"We'll take Luther back to Tombstone," Behan said. "Rest of you can follow on, see if you can't run down these other fellas."

"Behan and all his deputies?" Wyatt said.

"Under heavy guard," Virgil murmured.

"I'm sorry about your wife, Mr. Holliday," Luther said.

Doc grinned at him. "Kate ain't my wife," he said. "She wasn't on the stage. She didn't get shot, and if she had, I wouldn't care."

King looked as if he, Holliday, had said too much too fast, but Doc was already turning his horse, the shotgun back in the saddle scabbard under his leg. His shoulders shook. It might have been laughter, Wyatt knew. Or he might have been coughing.

Twenty-one

Propped against his saddle, Holliday wrote by fire-light in a small notebook.

"You writing about our thrilling adventures, Doc?" Wyatt said. "Sell it to one of those magazines in New York City."

"I'm writing a letter to my cousin," Holliday said.

"You got a cousin can read?" Morgan said.

"This one can," Holliday said. "She's a nun."

"Goddamn," Morgan said. "A nun? You a papist, Doc?"

"She is," Holliday said. "And I don't want to hear anything about it."

Morgan shrugged. There was a thin rasp in Holliday's voice that Morgan recognized. Doc sure did have a hair trigger.

"You telling her about us heroic lawmen?" Doc snorted.

"I'm telling her that I'll mail this tomorrow because I'm hauling my sore ass back into Tombstone," he said, "instead of chasing around in these mountains like a goddamned fool."

"Quitting, Doc?" Virgil said.

"You're goddamned right I am," Doc said. "We ain't going to catch Billy Leonard or anybody else riding around these mountains. I'm going back and wait for them to show up."

"He's right," Masterson said. "I'm a little saddle sore myself."

"You're getting soft, Bat," Wyatt said.

"I'm getting smart," Masterson said. "We're just in the foothills and we're low on food. You want to wander around out here, until you run out altogether, God bless you. I'm going to get a bath and a hot meal and maybe a whore."

"We'll resupply at Joe Hill's ranch," Virgil said.

"Resupply my ass," Holliday said. "Hill's in with the rustlers as much as Len Redfield."

"Sure," Wyatt said. "But he'll sell us food."

"I'm going back with Doc," Masterson said and rolled over in his blankets, with his back to the fire.

"Free country," Virgil said.

One by one, the posse dropped off to sleep, leaving only Holliday still sitting up by the fire writing in his notebook. The next morning, he and Masterson saddled up right after breakfast and rode their tired horses at an easy pace west toward Tombstone.

Two days later, Johnny Behan, with Billy Breakenridge and Buckskin Frank Leslie to track, caught up with the Earp posse in the valley of the San Simon River near the New Mexico border.

"King busted out," Breakenridge told them, laughing, while Behan was ahead with Leslie looking for sign. "Henry Jones was drawing up a bill of sale for King's horse to John Dunbar, and King went out the back door, mounted up and rode away."

"Who had him?" Virgil asked.

"Harry Woods," Breakenridge said. "Standing right there."

"Amazing that Harry didn't see him go," Virgil said.

"Amazing," Breakenridge said.

"Amazing that a horse happened to be saddled out back," Virgil said.

"Amazing."

"We'll be out awhile," Virgil said. "Somebody ought to go back and look for King."

He looked at Breakenridge.

"Billy?"

Breakenridge shook his head.

"I'm with Johnny," he said.

"Why not Johnny?" Morgan said. "He's the damn sheriff."

Virgil smiled and shook his head without saying anything.

"Johnny won't go," Wyatt said.

"It should be you, Wyatt," Virgil said. "You're the best of us anyway."

Wyatt nodded.

"How long you planning to be out?"

Virgil shrugged.

"A week if we're lucky, maybe more. See what Johnny says."

"He's talking 'bout a week," Breakenridge said.

"Luther's got a two-day start on me, three at least by the time I get to Tombstone."

"What I don't want," Virgil said, "is for Luther to be swaggering around town making us look like a bunch of goddamned jackasses."

Wyatt nodded.

"If he's around town," Wyatt said, "I'll make sure he don't swagger."

He and Virgil grinned at each other. Then Wyatt turned his horse and rode slowly away, toward Tombstone, thinking about Josie Marcus. There was nothing new in that. He thought about Josie Marcus most of the time.

"A week," he said to the chestnut gelding he was riding. The horse's ears moved slightly. "A goddamned week."

Twenty-two

Wearing a freshly laundered shirt, bathed and clean-shaven and smelling of bay rum, Wyatt knocked on Josie Marcus's door on a pleasant March evening, just getting dark and lyrical with the sound of desert bird-song.

"Wyatt," she said.

"Evening, Josie."

"I thought you were with the posse."

"Posse's still out," Wyatt said. "I came back to see about Luther King."

Josie smiled.

"He's not here," she said.

"Neither is Johnny," Wyatt said.

"Why, so he isn't," she said, and smiled.

"May I come in?"

"Yes," Josie said. "You may."

She stepped aside and held the door, and he took off his hat and walked into the small living room that looked out onto Third Street.

"Would you like coffee?" she said.

"Yes, please," Wyatt said.

He waited while she went into the kitchen and made the coffee. The room was silent.

Third Street was far enough from the center of town so that there was no street sound, except the occasional sound of a horse going slowly by. There were flowers in a pottery vase on the table by the window.

Josie returned with two cups of coffee in saucers on a small wooden tray. She handed one cup and saucer to Wyatt.

"Won't you sit?" she said, and nodded toward a straight-backed wooden chair with curved arms and an upholstered back, which must have been freighted in from San Francisco.

He sat, carefully so as not to spill the coffee.

"Have you had any luck finding Luther King?" she asked.

Wyatt smiled.

"Luther's probably in Mexico by now," Wyatt said.

"I see. Will you be rejoining the posse?"

Again Wyatt smiled.

"No," he said. "I don't think I will."

"Do you know when they'll be back?"

"Be out another week for sure," Wyatt said.

This time it was Josie who smiled.

"Did you really come back to look for Luther King?" Josie said.

"If I'd seen him, I'd have collared him."

"But you didn't, and now you're here," Josie said. "Did you plan to collar me?"

Wyatt drank coffee, and put the cup back down carefully in the saucer, and looked up at her. His face was serious.

"Well, yes," he said. "In a manner of speaking."

There was a little more color in Josie's face, he thought, and maybe she was breathing a little quicker, but it was hard to see because it was nearly dark out and Josie had not lit a lamp. She didn't say anything for a moment. Then she stood and picked up the two cups and saucers and put them on the tray and carried them without a word into the kitchen. He heard her put the tray on the kitchen table. Then she came back into the room, walking quite briskly. He stood, afraid she was going to show him the door, but she didn't. She walked right up to him and put her body against his and raised her face and said in the softest voice imaginable, "I'll go peacefully."

In the bedroom it was a blur of discarded clothing and tangled bedclothes, the smell of soap and perfume, the feel of her mouth, her body arching, hair, hands, thighs, the sound of her breathing, the sound of her voice, urgency, tension, strength, submission. Wyatt had been with women everywhere he went. He had never been with a woman like this. When it was over he lay as if stunned beside her on the bed in the now-dark room. Her head leaned against his chest.

"Mother of God," he said.

She moved her head on his chest and said nothing. He lay without thinking, still in the high wash of emotion slow to recede. A team went past on Third Street. He heard the creak of harness and the sound of the horses. He felt as if he had walked through a passage into a country he'd never seen, and from which he could never return.

"It is all different now," he said.

She moved her head again, only a little, on his chest. Slowly thought came back. Would it always be like this? Probably not. But it could always be good. Was it like this with Behan? No. What about Mattie?

"So what do we do, Josie?"

"I don't know."

"We have to be together."

"Yes."

And there it was. His life, which had been one thing this morning, was another thing tonight. She had to do something about Behan. He had to do something about Mattie. Mattie would be hurt. Behan would be angry. Maybe there'd be trouble. But that was only incidental. The shape of his future was now set; he knew in ways he could never articulate, could never understand or even think about, that the possibility which had begun to assemble when he'd first seen her face in *Pinafore on Wheels,* perhaps the only insubstantial possibility that he had ever allowed himself to entertain, had coalesced in this moment of frantic unification, and become no longer possibility, but the singular determinant of the rest of his life.

"It'll stir up a lot of trouble," Wyatt said.

"I don't care," Josie said.

"No," Wyatt said, "I don't either."

"So we might as well make the most of it," Josie said and kissed him, and he rolled toward her and the future once again surged over them.

Twenty-three

"Allie's pretty mad," Virgil said. "Told me she didn't want you coming to the house no more."

"She knows about Josie," Wyatt said.

Virgil drank some beer and put the glass down and wiped his mustache on his sleeve.

"Everybody in the damn town knows," Virgil said.

Wyatt nodded slowly, looking into his coffee cup.

"Including Mattie," he said.

"What you going to do about Mattie?" Virgil said.

"Damned if I know," Wyatt said. "She won't leave, and I can't throw her out. She can't take care of herself."

"No," Virgil said.

"Couple of days," Wyatt said, "she'd be in a crib east of Sixth Street."

"I know," Virgil said. "Maybe you could move out on her."

"She'd follow me," Wyatt said.

Virgil nodded. He was drawing little circles with the bottom of his beer mug on the wet table-top.

"Besides," Wyatt said, "it's my house."

"Yep."

"What you going to do about Allie?"

Virgil kept drawing his little circles while he looked across the room and out through the half-doors into Allen Street.

"I told her my brothers would always be welcome in my house."

"How she like that?"

"She said to me that it was her house too, and she didn't marry no goddamned brothers, she married me."

Wyatt smiled.

"Tough, ain't she," he said.

"Yeah, and good-hearted. She feels bad for Mattie."

"Hell, Virgil, I feel bad for Mattie, but there isn't anything I can do about it."

"You could give up Josie," Virgil said carefully.

"No," Wyatt said, "I couldn't."

Virgil continued to look out at Allen Street. It was not the kind of conversation he enjoyed.

"Guess maybe I understand that," he said after a while. "Not so sure I could give up Allie either."

"I don't want to give you and Allie no trouble," Wyatt said. "I can stay away from your house."

Virgil shook his head, and looked, for the first time in the conversation, straight at his younger brother.

"No," Virgil said, " 'less you stop being my brother, or it stops being my house, you are welcome. Allie understands it. She don't like it, but she will do what I say about this. You come over just like always. There won't be no trouble."

Wyatt nodded.

"What about Behan?" Virgil said.

"House belongs to Josie," Wyatt said. "Her father paid for it."

"So Johnny'll have to get out?"

"Looks that way."

"Makes him look like a fool," Virgil said.

"Wasn't my intention," Wyatt said.

"It don't help us in town to have this happen," Virgil said. "It don't help us to have Johnny Behan against us, either."

"I can deal with Johnny," Wyatt said.

"He won't come straight at you."

"No."

"But it don't mean he won't come," Virgil said.

"Or send somebody," Wyatt said.

They were quiet together for a time. Listening to the saloon sounds. The click of glasses, the low murmur of the men at card games. The sound of booted feet. An occasional high laugh from one of the whores who worked the saloons.

"Whoever he sends," Virgil said, "they got to go up against you and me and Morgan—and Holliday, I guess, if he's sober enough to shoot."

"Can't recall," Wyatt said, "Doc ever being too drunk to shoot."

"True enough," Virgil said. "The skinny bastard can do that, can't he."

"It may not come to much," Wyatt said. "Johnny's a pretty careful fella. Wants to get ahead."

"Man doesn't get ahead, around here, at least," Virgil said. "Being made to look like a horse's ass in public."

"Maybe Johnny don't know that," Wyatt said.

Twenty-four

Mattie sat in the kitchen in a straight chair with a water glass of whiskey in her hand and tears coming down her face. She didn't look at Wyatt.

"Don't you want your breakfast?"

Wyatt shook his head. He was standing in the doorway holding a rifle, its muzzle pointed at the floor.

"I had breakfast with Morgan," he said. "I just stopped in to pick up the Winchester."

"I cooked it special for you," she said. "Got some fresh eggs from Vita Coleman."

She sniffed and wiped her nose with the sleeve of her dress.

"Christ," Wyatt said, "do you cry in your sleep?"

Mattie shook her head and drank from her glass, her eyes fixed on the front of the iron stove across the room.

"If you're hoping for sympathy, Mattie, I haven't got any left. I'm doing what I have to do."

"I'm not leaving you," Mattie said. "If you go, I'll follow you."

"For what?"

"I'm your wife."

"You're not even that, not really. We never took any vows."

"I'm your wife," she said.

"You're a damned drunk," Wyatt said. "It's still morning and you're already drunk."

"I'm only doing what you make me do," Mattie said. "I can't bear the pain without it."

Wyatt took in a big breath of air and let it out slowly.

"Mattie," he said. "That's bullshit and you know it. You been drinking most of the time, long as I knew you. It used to be sherry. Now it's whiskey. But the drinking ain't new."

"I got nothing else to do," Mattie said. "I'm alone all the time. You're never home."

Her face was bunched up as if trying to be smaller. She was pale except for a red flush over her cheekbones. She drank again from the whiskey glass.

"Why would I want to come home?" Wyatt said. "Watch you cry and drink whiskey."

Mattie didn't answer. Her eyes were squeezed nearly shut. She had slept on top of the bed in the dress she was still wearing. She looked at the stove as if to penetrate the black iron with her narrow, wet gaze.

"I won't give you up," she said without inflection.

"Jesus Christ," Wyatt said and turned and went through the parlor and out the front door.

Carrying the Winchester, Wyatt walked up Fremont Street, his boots making soft sounds in the thick dirt. The morning sun was behind him and his shadow spilled out in front of him, angular and much too long. It was already warm, and the sky was high and cloudless. He turned up Fourth Street, past Spangenberg's Gun Shop on his left, and on the other side, farther up, at the corner of Allen Street, the Can Can Restaurant where he had had breakfast with Charlie Shibell and talked of being a deputy. Long time ago, Wyatt thought. He turned right on Allen past Hafford's. Across the street, Johnny Behan came out of the Grand Hotel; he saw Wyatt and waved. Wyatt touched his hat brim and kept going. Johnny was a genial man. Careful about giving offense. *He won't come straight at you,* Virgil had said. *But it don't mean he won't come.* Hell, maybe he was glad to get away from Josie. Wyatt smiled to himself. Be goddamned glad, myself, if Mattie would run off with somebody.

Twenty-five

The way the moonlight fell in the room, he could see Josie's face as they lay together in her dark bedroom. Her eyes seemed very large in the pale light.

"You're very strong," Josie said. "I feel it when we're doing sex."

"We're all strong," Wyatt said. "James too, 'fore he got shot up."

"In the war?"

"Yep."

"Yankee?"

"Yep. Illinois."

"He doesn't seem dangerous like his brothers," Josie said. Her voice had an affectionate teasing sound.

"Oh, James will fight if he has to, best he can with that shoulder. But he's an easygoing boy. I think James's done most of the shooting he wants to do already."

"How 'bout you?" Josie said.

He loved the sound her voice made in the dark room. "I don't mind shooting," Wyatt said.

"The men say you are a very good shooter."

"I practice," Wyatt said. "Mostly in the morning, early. You don't get good just packing a gun around. You need to work at it."

"Can you draw very fast?"

"That's the dime novel guff," Wyatt said. "Fast ain't anywhere near as important as steady."

"I should think you'd want to get off the first shot."

"Mostly I'd want to hit what I shot at," Wyatt said.

"Well," Josie said. "You're still here. I guess the proof is in the pudding."

"Never mind about my pudding," Wyatt said, and they both giggled.

"I'm not sure I ever heard you laugh before," Josie said. "I certainly never heard you laugh like that."

"I'm a little different than usual," Wyatt said, "when I'm with you."

"You're pretty different," she said, and they both laughed again. "I heard that your friend Holliday was involved in the Benson stage holdup."

"That's just talk," Wyatt said.

"I heard he was a friend of Billy Leonard's," Josie said.

As they talked Wyatt ran his hands lightly over her body beneath the covers.

"Doc knew him in Las Vegas," Wyatt said.

Josie rubbed her cheek against his shoulder and shivered slightly as his hands moved over her.

"Don't mean he helped him hold up the stage."

"I even heard you boys did it," Josie said.

"It's cowboy talk," Wyatt said.

"So who do you think did it?"

"Billy Leonard, Harry Head, and Jim Crane," Wyatt said. "Like Len Redfield told us."

"You know them?"

Her face was close to his. As she talked, he could feel her lips brush his very lightly.

"Uh-huh," Wyatt said. "Rustlers. Len Redfield too, and his brother. Tight with the Clantons. They all ride with Ringo and Curley Bill."

"I heard Curley Bill got shot," Josie said.

"Up in Galeyville, fella named Jim Wallace, a shooter from over Lincoln County. Put one into Bill's cheek, took out one of his teeth."

"Oh, poor man."

"Yes," Wyatt said. "I was Wallace, I wouldn't like my prospects."

"I meant Bill," she said.

"Oh. Well, Bill'll get over it, probably better than Wallace will."

She shifted slightly against him as his hands continued to move over her.

"Lot of people think you did it, Wyatt. Say Marshal Williams tipped you to the big payload. Even on the posse, people say you and Virgil were just leading them around in circles."

"Josie, we wasn't doing the tracking. Billy Breakenridge was doing it first. Then Frank Leslie come out. He was doing the tracking. None of us can track like Frank."

"I . . . don't . . . care," she said, trying to keep her breathing steady, "if . . . you . . . did."

"Well," Wyatt said, "I didn't."

His hands moved firmly now, and she pressed against him, squirming a little.

"You . . . think . . . Johnny . . . might be . . . spreading rumors . . . because . . . ?"

"Because of us?"

Her breathing was so heavy now that it was hard for her to speak, and when she did it sounded very much like gasping.

"Yes."

"Could be," Wyatt said, and she arched against him and her mouth covered his and they stopped talking.

CHRONICLE

Henry Wadsworth Longfellow dies . . . Jesse James dies . . . Ralph Waldo Emerson dies . . . Richard Wagner's *Parsifal* is performed.

* * *

CHRISTIAN TEMPERANCE UNION

October 26—

At Waltham, in the Universalist Church, yesterday, was held a convention of The Woman's Christian Temperance Union of Middlesex county. In the morning devotional exercises were engaged in, Mrs. E. T. Luce presiding. In the afternoon Mrs. Talbot of Malden was in the chair, and there was a general discussion of the temperance question. Mr. R. B. Johnson presided in the evening when Mrs. R. W. McLaughlin delivered an excellent temperance address. The gathering was a large one, most of the unions being represented.

* * *

**THE HARVARD FOOTBALL ELEVEN
DEFEATS THE "TECHS"**
October 26—
The Harvard eleven won its second victory from the
Institute of Technology team, yesterday afternoon, on
Holmes field, in the presence of a fair number of spec-
tators.

* * *

AMERICAN MARINES AT ALEXANDRIA
London, October 25—
At a civic dinner here last night, Lord Charles Beresford,
who commanded the gunboat Condor, which took part in
the bombardment of Alexandria, in describing events oc-
curring after the bombardment, characterized the American Marines at Alexandria as brave fellows. He said they
rendered valuable assistance in saving many buildings during the conflagration.

* * *

REPORTS OF THE SUPERINTENDENT

OF THE YELLOWSTONE PARK

Washington, October 25—

P. H. Conger, superintendent of the Yellowstone National Park submitted his report to the Secretary of the Interior today. He says that hunting has been practically suspended, and deer and elk are no longer killed. He regards the salary paid assistant superintendents as too small. He suggests that the law dividing the responsibility of the government of the park between the War and Interior departments be changed so as to place the park under the interior department. The hotel built by Rufus Hatch & Co. is completed, and is represented as commodious and well kept.

* * *

NIHILISTIC STUDENTS ARRESTED

St. Petersburg, October 25—

Arrests of Nihilists continue daily. Today a number of students were arrested and upon the person of one of them was found a manifesto headed "Executive Committee to the Czar." The document demands general amnesty for political offenders, entire freedom of the press and speech, and a parliament elected by the people. Unless

these demands are complied with the writer threatens re-
bellion, vengeance upon the nobility and the death of the
Czar.

* * *

MILWAUKEE BEER
*From the celebrated Joseph Schlitz Brewing Company Milwau-
kee, Wis. for sale in half or quarter bottles or in bottles bearing
my trade-mark and name.*

Joseph Gahm
83 Commercial Street

* * *

MEN WITH A SWEET TOOTH
*Said the young blonde in attendance at the candy counter in
Macy's: "Oh yes indeed, many gentlemen buy candy here and
from the fact that they eat from the package, and tell us it is for
themselves, I believe they have a sweet tooth and like candy as
much as we girls."*

Twenty-six

It was the beginning of June. Wyatt stood at an open window in the office of Earp/Winders Mining trying to find a breeze. Behind him with his shirtsleeves rolled and his collar unbuttoned Virgil sat at a rolltop desk with his feet up, occasionally wiping sweat off his face with a blue handkerchief. In the shade of the overhang downstairs in front of the Crystal Palace the temperature registered at 104.

"Hear Johnny's been coming around after Josie," Virgil said.

"Yeah. It's her house. She's told him she don't want to see him, but he comes around some anyways."

"Going to do anything about that?"

Wyatt smiled.

"Morgan maybe done it for me," he said.

"Oh?"

A freight wagon pulled by six sweat-darkened mules labored past, heading east up Allen Street. There were three whiskey barrels standing upright and lashed side by side to the back of the driver's seat.

"I was up in Tucson couple weeks back, with Winders, about that new shaft extension on the Mountain Maid. I knew Johnny'd been after Josie about letting him back in, so I asked Morgan to keep an eye on her. You know Morgan wants to be a tough nut like his brothers."

Virgil smiled.

"He is a tough nut," Virgil said.

"Like his brothers," Wyatt said.

"'Cept maybe a little too quick sometimes," Virgil said, "proving it."

"Hell, Virg, you remember when you was his age."

Virgil grinned again. "I was never his age. What'd he do?"

"Well, Josie told me that Morgan came by, said he was going to sort of sit around for a while, case Johnny showed up and bothered her. So she gave him some coffee and they sat in the living room and they talked. You know Morgan."

"He could talk to a sage chicken," Virgil said.

"Yep, and then sure enough, Johnny comes knocking at the door and Josie lets him in, and there's Morg sitting there with his coffee. Well, Johnny says, 'What the hell is he doing there?' And Morgan says he's keeping company with his brother's girlfriend. And Johnny tells him to get out of his house, and Josie reminds him it ain't Johnny's house. It's her house paid for by her father, and Johnny says it don't give her the right to live in it and be a slut for the Earps. So Morgan knocks him down, and Johnny gets up, and Josie says Morgan was annoyed as hell. 'I'm losing my goddamned punch,' he says, and knocks Johnny down again, and this time Johnny stays down for a while, and when he gets up, sort of tottering, Morgan runs him out the front door."

"Good, Johnny wasn't packing," Virgil said.

"Wouldn't matter if he was," Wyatt said. "He wouldn't jerk on Morgan."

"You never know," Virgil said. "You never know how far you can push somebody."

A single rider with a big hat and a checkered blue shirt rode a lathered chestnut horse up Fifth Street and turned the corner. He reined and got off the horse in front of the Oriental across Fifth Street from the Crystal Palace. He led the horse down to the watering trough in front of the Arcade and let him drink. Then he brought the chestnut back and tied him to the rack in front of the Oriental and went in.

"Josie thinks it's Johnny doing most of the talking about Doc holding up the stage," Wyatt said.

"Be a way to get at you," Virgil said.

"Sort of roundabout, ain't it?" Wyatt said.

"Johnny's a roundabout guy," Virgil said.

Wyatt nodded, as much to himself as to Virgil. Below the

window, three whores walked up Allen Street toward Sixth Street carrying groceries. Wyatt recognized them. They worked for Nosey Kate Lowe. They'd have an early supper at Nosey Kate's and get ready for work.

"I was to find Leonard, Head and Crane," Wyatt said. "Might sort of settle the question."

"Guess it would," Virgil said. "You got an idea how you're going to do that?"

"Well, they're someplace," Wyatt said.

"Guess so," Virgil said.

"And somebody knows where."

"Specifying who?" Virgil said.

"Well, I'd be willing to bet Ike Clanton knows."

"Ike rides with the cowboys. Him and the McLaurys," Virgil said. "You think Ike will turn in his friends to help you?"

"Sure," Wyatt said. "Make it worth his while."

"He don't like us," Virgil said.

"I ain't going to ask him to do it 'cause he likes us."

"What you got to offer him?"

"I'll think of something," Wyatt said.

"I expect you will," Virgil said. "Just don't get yourself in a position where you got to trust Ike."

"Not likely," Wyatt said. "But maybe I can get Leonard and the boys to trust Ike."

"Be a stupid thing for them to do," Virgil said.

"Which one of them three boys you figure to be the smartest?" Wyatt said.

Virgil grinned.

"I'd say none of them."

"That sounds right to me," Wyatt said.

Twenty-seven

Wyatt and Ike Clanton had a drink together at the Oriental in the late afternoon with the heat still oppressive. Ike was drinking whiskey with a beer chaser. Wyatt nursed a cup of coffee. Ike was a fancy-looking man, Wyatt thought. Curly hair and a tricky little Vandyke beard. His mouth seemed somehow loose as he talked, and the fine network of broken veins that spidered his sun-darkened face suggested how much beer and whiskey he'd drunk in a lifetime of ranch work and saloons.

"I want the credit for capturing those three boys," Wyatt said. "Be a big help to me if I run for sheriff, and it'll take the pressure off Doc."

"Meaning you'll get them to confess and it'll clear Doc's name," Clanton said.

He had on a white cotton shirt. He had rolled the sleeves up and unbuttoned the collar. Sweat was glossy on his neck and his bare arms. He swallowed a shot of whiskey and some beer.

"That's about right," Wyatt said.

"But I get the reward," Clanton said.

"You get them back here where I can grab them and you get the money."

"Secret."

"If that's how you want it," Wyatt said.

"If I was to do this at all," Clanton said, "it's got to be that way. They ride with Brocius and Ringo. They was to find out I turned them boys in, I ain't got a snowball's chance in hell of living to spend the money."

"Nobody will know," Wyatt said. "Except my brothers."

"Say I go over there," Clanton said. "With Joe Hill, maybe Frank McLaury, and we get these boys to come back. And we get them out of New Mexico and bring them to, say, Frank's ranch. Then what?"

"Then I'm waiting with a posse and we take them and you get the reward money."

"They'll make a fight," Clanton said. "You're going to have to kill them."

Wyatt shrugged.

"How do I know Wells Fargo will pay the reward if they're dead?"

"You got my word," Wyatt said.

"No offense, but I don't know if Wells Fargo will stand by your word."

"I'll get a telegram," Wyatt said. "I'll have Marshal Williams put it in writing that they pay for Leonard, Head, and Crane or their corpses."

Ike poured more whiskey into his shot glass and drank it off, then drank the rest of his beer and motioned toward the barman that he wanted another one.

"I'd just as soon see Billy Leonard out of the way," he said. "I got a ranch in New Mexico that he says is his and he won't give it up."

"So you get the reward money and settle the, ah, land dispute," Wyatt said.

Clanton drank again. He looked at Earp over the glass rim as he did. Hard man to figure, Ike thought. His face never showed anything. He never seemed to say more than he had to. You always had the sense that he had some cards held back and that what you were talking about was only part of what he was thinking.

"How do I know you're leveling with me?" Ike said.

"You don't," Earp said.

There seemed to be no change in his expression or any difference in the way he was talking, but something about the way Earp said "You don't" made the pit of Ike's stomach tighten. When he was scared it made him angry, and when he was angry he drank more and talked more and louder. He half knew that, but he couldn't stop it.

"Maybe you are partners with those boys like they say," Ike said. "Maybe you got the money and you want them to come in so you can kill them while you are arresting them. Then they can't peach on you and you got all the cash."

Earp was silent, looking at him without expression. It made Ike more uncomfortable. He had some more whiskey.

"That could be, couldn't it, Wyatt? What you got to say about that?"

"You want the deal or not?" Earp said.

Ike's stomach clenched tighter.

"I got to think on it," he said. "Talk to Frank and Joe. Virgil know about this?"

"Yes."

"Might want to talk to him."

"Do that," Earp said.

"I will," Ike said. "I will. I can't just do it because you say so, you know? These people are friends of mine. I got to give it some thought. I got to talk to people."

"Not too many people, Ike."

"I'll talk to whoever I damn want," Ike said.

"I expect you will," Earp said. "Might not be a secret, though, time you get through."

Twenty-eight

It was hot and the river was low. The green belt along the San Pedro had narrowed as the water dropped. But there was some shade and there was a small breeze that drifted off the river. Josie and Wyatt spread a blanket in the best shade the sparse cottonwoods provided and put out some food. Canned ham, cold biscuits, canned peaches. Far enough away so they wouldn't feel it, squatting on his heels, with his sleeves rolled, Wyatt built a fire and made coffee with water dipped from the river. He wore no coat. He wore no handgun, but there was a Winchester behind the seat in the buckboard. His chest where his shirt was open was white, as were his forearms. His face and neck and hands were weathered in sharp contrast. When they had eaten, and put the dishes and leftover food in a sack in the back of the buckboard, they sat beside the river leaning against a tree trunk and drank sweet, strong black coffee from tin cups.

"You ever think about moving on?" Josie said.

"Not without you," Wyatt said.

"No," Josie said. "Not without me."

Wyatt had unharnessed the horses and tethered them a little downriver at the water's edge. The horses stayed in the shade, drinking now and then from the river, and cropping at the sparse green buffalo grass. They twitched their skin occasionally the way horses do to shake off flies, and swished their tails sporadically for the same purpose.

"Maybe someday," Wyatt said.

"Why not now?"

"Not rich yet," Wyatt said.

"We could go to San Francisco," Josie said. "You could get rich there."

Across the river a coyote stopped in a splash of sunshine and stared at them calmly, then loped on.

"It's a city," Wyatt said. "None of the things I'm good at will make you rich in a city."

"You could be a policeman."

Wyatt smiled and shook his head.

"You're a policeman here, sometimes," Josie said. "You've been a policeman in Dodge City and Wichita and . . . where, Ellsworth?"

"San Francisco," Wyatt said, "the captain tells you what to do and the lieutenant tells you what to do and the sergeant tells you what to do."

He shook his head again. Josie leaned her head against his shoulder. His shirt was damp with sweat.

"So what are you so good at here?" she said. "Doing what you want to?"

"Yes."

"When you're Virgil's deputy, doesn't he tell you what to do?"

"He's my brother."

"That makes it different?"

"Means he's asking. He's got a right to ask."

"But no strangers."

Wyatt shrugged and drank some of his coffee.

"What else you good at, staying here?" Josie said.

"I can shoot," Wyatt said.

"Uh-huh."

"And I like being where it's not so crowded," he said. "I'm a farm boy, you know, from Illinois."

"Would you ever want a ranch?"

"Maybe someday. Right now I'm a town man. I got interests in saloons and mines."

"Not a city man," Josie said. Her voice had a happy, teasing quality to it that he liked. "And not a cowboy. A town man. Right in the middle, I guess."

"Right in the middle," Wyatt said.

"Then I guess that's where I am," Josie said. "Right in the middle."

Wyatt smiled at her.

"How'd you get so good at shooting?" Josie said.

"We're doing it backwards," Wyatt said, smiling. "First we fall in love, then we learn about each other."

"So how?" Josie said.

"Lot of men can be good at shooting, they practice enough."

"Anybody?"

"Not anybody. You got to have sort of the feel for it. Your hand and your eye need to connect in the right way."

"And yours do."

"Yep. Must be in the blood. All of us do. James before he got hurt. Virgil, Morgan, Warren, too, I suspect."

"I haven't even met Warren."

"He's the baby," Wyatt said. "I imagine he'll be along."

"All the Earps," Josie said.

"You can trust family."

"So do you practice more than most men?"

"Probably."

"Why?"

Wyatt was quiet for a while, looking at the way the sun filtered through the overhanging trees and danced on the still surface of the barely moving river. Josie shifted slightly to be more comfortable. The place where their bodies touched was damp, but neither one cared. They were used to hot as they were used to cold, and both conditions were simply part of the natural order.

"If you come to something natural," Wyatt said finally,

"and it's something that can be put to use, I always figured you ought to polish it up, best you can."

She thought about that. Something rustled briefly along the riverbank and went into the water with a splash.

"Have you killed many people?"

"No."

"But some?"

"Yes."

"Do you mind?"

Again Wyatt looked at the river. The surface of the water was smooth. Whatever had gone into the river had disappeared without a ripple. Wyatt usually did what he thought he should do, and moved on. Josie was asking questions he had not thought about. It was hard to think about them now, and harder to put them into words. But Josie wanted to know, and he would tell her.

"I've never taken any pleasure in it," Wyatt said. "But if it needs to be done, I'm willing to do it, and when it's done, it don't bother me much afterwards."

"Do you remember your first gun?"

"You mean the first one I shot?"

"Yes."

"I suppose it was one of my father's. He was provost during the war. James and Virgil was gone to the war, and Warren was still little, but me and Morgan used to steal a big old Colt forty-four from my father's room and sneak off and shoot it. It was a percussion cap pistol, Dragoon model, and we'd shoot a thousand rebs at once with it at the far back end of the cornfield."

"Could you hit anything with it?"

"Not much. It was too big a gun for us."

"Your father ever catch you?"

"Nope. I suspect he didn't want to. I'm pretty sure he knew. Be hard shooting off a forty-four Colt around our cornfield without somebody noticing."

"And you liked shooting it."

"Sure."

"Why?"

"I don't know exactly. Lotta people like it. You ever fire a handgun, Josie?"

"No."

"Well, there's a lot of power there. You squeeze off a shot and you feel it." Wyatt made an enlarging gesture with his hands. "You create it out of nothing . . . right there in your hand."

"And it makes you powerful."

"Yes," Wyatt said. "It does."

Twenty-nine

"*Things are looking* up," Virgil said. "Ben Sippy skedaddled, and I'm the acting city marshal."

The two men leaned on the hitching rail outside the Oriental.

"Skedaddled?" Wyatt said.

"Uh-huh."

"Not just away visiting for a couple of weeks?"

"Clum says there's money missing."

"Ahhh," Wyatt said.

He was dressed for work in a dark suit and a starched white shirt.

"You going to be around?" Virgil said.

"Sure, I'm dealing here, doing some undercover work for Wells Fargo, me and Morgan. I'll be around, you need a special deputy."

Virgil nodded. Wyatt waited. He knew Virgil. There was something else. Half a dozen miners, off shift, passed them and turned into the Oriental.

"What's going on with you and Mattie?" Virgil said.

"Hearing about it at home?" Wyatt said.

Virgil smiled.

"You're with Josie," Virgil said, "but you're still living with Mattie."

"It's my house," Wyatt said. "I'm not going to leave it."

"And Mattie won't?"

"She won't," Wyatt said.

"You and she still . . . ah, there any poontang there?"

"Hell no," Wyatt said. "I sleep in the front room."

Virgil nodded.

"Guess you can't just throw her out," Virgil said.

"No. I threatened it one night and she said if I did she'd just sit outside the house all day."

"Wouldn't help much, next sheriff's election," Virgil said.

"Nope."

The two men looked at each other a moment.

"Sorry if it's causing trouble with Allie," Wyatt said.

"Can't be helped," Virgil said. "You can't stay with Mattie just 'cause Allie wants you to."

"I didn't think Allie liked Mattie," Wyatt said.

"She don't." Virgil took his hat off and fanned his face with it. "Hot as hell, ain't it?"

"Better get used to it," Wyatt said. "That's where we're all headed."

Virgil grinned at him and put his hat back on.

"Guess I'll walk around town," he said. "You got them miners in there getting drunk, waiting for you to fleece 'em."

"That's what they were sent here for," Wyatt said. Virgil strolled down Allen Street. Wyatt turned and went into the cooler dimness of the saloon.

At the bar Denny McCann nodded at him. Ike Clanton was there, too, with whiskey in front of him. He ignored Wyatt. Wyatt went to the faro table and sat down. Three miners came over directly, carrying their drinks, and sat down with him. Wyatt shuffled and spread the first layout of the evening. He liked dealing faro. He found it relaxing. He had good hands and calmness. The game could engage his attention without demanding it. His reputation kept most of the players in check, and he could think about Josie and the time to come. The house won, of course, and he took a percentage of the winnings.

At the bar, McCann, lean and pale in a dark suit, was talking to a thin-faced little prostitute named Fancy. Down the bar Ike Clanton had drunk enough whiskey to loosen his mouth. He sidled down the bar and put an arm around Fancy's waist and said something. She turned away from him. He moved after her. McCann said something to Ike, and Ike shoved Fancy aside. Wyatt watched with interest while he fanned out another hand of faro. Ike and McCann stood facing each other, McCann a good three inches taller than Ike.

"You think I'm scared of you, you prettified, goddamned dandy boy," Ike said.

His speech was slurred. McCann slapped him hard across the face and it staggered Ike. The room went quiet. One of the bartenders moved down the bar toward them. The other men at the bar moved away from them. Fancy dodged out of the way and looked over at Wyatt. McCann kept his pale-eyed stare right on Ike, and Clanton reacted as he always did.

"You sonova bitch," he said when he got himself steadied. "Arm yourself and be ready. I'll look for you on Allen Street."

Then Ike pushed himself off the bar and rushed out, banging against the doorjamb with his right shoulder. McCann looked after him for a time and then leaned over the bar and put out his hand. The bartender handed him a Colt revolver with a walnut handle. McCann checked to see that it was loaded and left the bar.

At the next table Fred Dodge turned to Wyatt.

"Ike's going for a gun," he said.

"Go tell Virgil," Wyatt said. "'Less they do it in here, it's his job."

Fred looked blankly at Wyatt for a moment, then stood and ran out the front door. Everyone else, including the faro players, crowded to the door after him trying to watch and stay out of the line of fire. Wyatt put the cards away, took his own Colt .45 from a drawer in the card table, stuck it in his belt, stood and pushed out through the crowd onto the boardwalk in front of the saloon. McCann waited motionless across Allen Street in front of the Wells Fargo office, his gambler's pallor more obvious in the harsh sunlight.

Ike rounded the corner of Fourth Street a block and a half from Denny McCann. He was carrying a handgun. He arrived at Fifth at almost the same moment that Virgil emerged from the Crystal Palace downstairs from his office. Virgil fell in beside Ike and matched his stride as they approached McCann together.

The street was quiet, and the people watching from the saloons were still.

Wyatt could hear Ike saying, "Stay out of this, Earp."

Virgil didn't answer. He was hatless and he wore no coat in the hundred-degree heat. Wyatt could see that he was heeled.

As they passed the front door of the Oriental, Virgil said, "Wyatt, I'm naming you a special deputy as of right now."

"Sure thing, Virg," Wyatt said.

When Ike and Virgil beside him came to a point about five feet from McCann, Ike stopped. Virgil moved between the two men.

"Can't have you boys shooting out here," Virgil said. "Put the guns away or I'll have to arrest you."

"Sonova bitch slapped me, Virgil. No man can do that and get away with it."

"Slap him back," Virgil said. "But you don't hand over that Colt, I'm going to have to take it."

McCann let his gun hang straight down by his side. But he didn't put it away.

"Piss on you, bluebelly," Clanton said. "All you Earps are bluebellies. You'd never stand by a cowboy."

He shoved Virgil. Thirty feet away on the boardwalk in front of the Oriental, Wyatt moved his coat aside and rested his right hand forward on his hip. Virgil rolled easily with the shove and slammed his left fist into Ike's face; at the same time he brought his right hand down hard on the barrel of Ike's gun and twisted it out of Ike's hand. Ike staggered backward. The punch had cut his lip, and he was bleeding freely. The blood ran down his chin and soaked into his shirt. As soon as he had Ike's gun, Virgil turned toward Denny McCann and put out his left hand.

"Give me the gun, Denny."

Holding his left forearm against his mouth, Ike fumbled into his pocket and came out with a jackknife. McCann handed his gun to Virgil.

From the boardwalk, Wyatt said, "Ike."

Ike turned and looked at Wyatt, still standing with his coat thrown back, his hand on his hip nearly touching his gun butt.

"Fucking bluebellies," Ike said.

He put the knife back in his pocket.

"There'll be another time, bluebellies," he said.

Then he turned and rushed back down Allen Street. Wyatt went back into the Oriental and sat at the faro table. He took the gun from his belt and put it back in the drawer and closed the drawer. Then he shuffled the cards and began to put down a new layout.

Thirty

They ran into each other having breakfast in the same cafe in Benson. Wyatt had finished some mining business and Johnny Ringo was finished with whatever business Johnny Ringo had. Now, full of coffee and bacon and fried sourdough, they were riding south together toward Tombstone.

The horses were allowed to drink their fill before they left Benson, and now in the hard, dry heat they were allowed to find their own pace. Wyatt was riding the same still-sound blue roan gelding he'd ridden north to Wichita from the buffalo fields. Ringo was on a gray horse with the flared nostrils and smallish head that hinted at Arabian ancestry.

"There's a lot of bad feelin' building," Ringo said. "Curley Bill don't like how you boys jumped him when Fred White got shot."

"Don't know why he would," Wyatt said.

The road was dry, and the horses kicked up dust with every step. On either side the desert vegetation seemed fossilized in the heat.

"Ike Clanton's been snarling and spitting like a wet bobcat since Virgil took up for Denny McCann."

"I think Virgil was takin' up for the law, John," Wyatt said.

"Prob'ly," Ringo said. "But it got Ike a split lip, and he ain't too good at seeing the differences among things."

"That's pretty much Ike's problem," Wyatt said.

He edged the blue roan left a bit with his right knee, to keep him from nosing Ringo's mare.

"Ike's pretty cinched in with Behan," Ringo said.

"Uh-huh."

"And so is Curley Bill," Ringo said.

"Uh-huh."

"And Behan's mad as hell at you."

"I expect he is," Wyatt said.

"Hope that girl's worth it," Ringo said.

"Miss Marcus," Wyatt said.

Ringo grinned. He was mostly an easy-tempered man, Wyatt thought. And even when he wasn't, he kept steady.

"Miss Marcus," Ringo said.

He was slimmer than Wyatt and not as tall, and he had a kind of gracefulness about him. Like a bullfighter. Wyatt had seen bullfights in Mexico. He hadn't liked them much, but he'd admired how quick and smooth the matadors were. Johnny Ringo reminded him of a matador. Everything was easy and graceful and much quicker than you thought it would be.

"She's worth it," Wyatt said.

The road went uphill, and the horses slowed. Ringo rode easily, relaxed in the saddle, his hands resting quietly on the pommel. He looked as if he could sleep on the horse if he had no one to talk with.

"I ride with Curley Bill," Ringo said.

"I know."

"Can't say I got much use for Ike. Seems to be mostly gut wind and mouth."

"That's Ike," Wyatt said.

"Got nothing against you Earps, either," Ringo said. "You're looking out for yourselves like the rest of us."

"We are," Wyatt said.

"And none of you is a back shooter."

"Nope."

"Which is more than I can say for Ike," Ringo said.

"I know."

"But Curley Bill and me . . ." Ringo thought a moment how he wanted to say it. "We look out for each other."

"Like me and my brothers," Wyatt said.

"Just like that," Ringo said. "So if there's trouble, and there will be if it's up to Behan . . ." Again Ringo paused, turning over what he'd say. "If there's trouble I got no choice," he said. "I'm with Bill."

"Can't be helped," Wyatt said.

"No," Ringo said. "It can't."

The sky was cloudless. The horses walked quietly beside

each other, heads half down, hooves muffled in the soft, dry dirt of the trail. In the desert heat, sweat evaporated from the riders almost the instant that it formed.

"Wish it could," Ringo said.

Wyatt said nothing.

Thirty-one

When Johnny Behan came to arrest Doc Holliday he came with six deputies, three with shotguns. Behan found Holliday at the bar of the Crystal Palace. It was the day after the Fourth, and Doc was nursing a hangover like most of Tombstone, including a sulky Big-Nose Katie Elder, who was also sporting a darkening bruise on her left cheekbone. She sat at a table across the room, not speaking to Doc. The deputies came in from the Fifth Street door and formed a ring around Holliday.

Behan stepped through the ring and said, "Doc, I have a warrant for your arrest."

Doc turned his back against the bar. He rested his elbows on the bar, a glass of whiskey in one hand, and stared at Behan.

"Fuck you," Doc said.

"There's an affidavit says you held up the Benson stage and killed Bud Philpot."

"Bullshit," Doc said.

Behan was watching his hands. Doc wouldn't stand a chance if he jerked on six men with their guns drawn, but Doc was crazy drunk and Behan knew it. They all knew it. Doc drank some whiskey.

"Warrant said you got to appear before the justice of the peace promptly."

"Whose affidavit is it?" Doc said.

The way Holliday was standing, his coat was open and Behan could see the butt of Doc's revolver. If he did decide to jerk on them, he might be quick enough to kill one of them before they cut him down. It would probably be Behan. Behan knew that, and so did the deputies.

"Big-Nose Kate's," Behan said.

Two bright spots of color appeared on Holliday's gray face. Behan found himself wishing that one of the Earps were there. They were the only friends Holliday had, and they had a calming influence on him. Maybe he should have let Virgil arrest him. The crime hadn't happened in Tombstone. It had happened outside the town in Behan's county and it was Behan's arrest, and everybody would have known it if he went to Virgil.

"That clap nest? She says I killed Bud Philpot? And you come for me with a fucking warrant because Big-Nose Whore says I did it?"

"You done it, Doc, you goddamned well know you done it."

Kate had come from her table and stood behind the ring of deputies. She was swaying slightly, and her tongue was thick.

"You killed Bud Philpot sure as I'm standing here," she said. It came out *shtanding*.

Holliday looked at her. His cheeks were bright red. His eyes were alive with something that made Behan uncomfortable. Despite the way he looked, Holliday's voice was as flat as tin when he spoke to her.

"I'm going to knock out every tooth in your ugly whore head," Holliday said.

"You already tried doing that, you peculiar bastard," Kate said. The remnants of her Hungarian accent lengthened the *a* and liquor slurred the *st*, and the word came out *Baashtaard*.

One of the deputies, Bill Breakenridge, said, "Why'nt you take that Colt out with your left hand, Doc, and put her on the bar and come on down to the jail."

"Why'nt you kiss my ass, Billy."

"I'll do that when you got the ten-gauge and I don't," Breakenridge said. "Put her on the bar, Doc."

Holliday didn't move.

"Shoot the sonova bitch," Kate said.

"Shut up, Kate," Breakenridge said pleasantly enough. He had the shotgun at his shoulder, aimed straight at Holliday.

"Come on, Doc," Behan said. "No need to be a hard case about this, somebody'll bail you out in a couple hours."

"Don't matter somebody bails me out when we get there," Holliday said. "I don't take orders from anybody, let alone a goose fucker like you, Johnny."

Behan flushed. He felt Doc's insane gaze on him. He realized suddenly what was disturbing in Holliday's eyes. Doc didn't care if he died or not. Behan felt the coldness of that sudden knowledge in his crotch. Nobody moved. Nobody seemed to know what to do. Behan felt the chill in his crotch spreading. He didn't know what to do either. Could they just cut him down here, right at the bar? If he gave the go-ahead to shoot, would Doc get him before he died? What would the Earps do if he killed Holliday? Why hadn't he thought all this out before he came in to the saloon? He could hear the silence building. He felt Doc's eyes on him. When someone spoke behind him, he jumped visibly and hated himself for jumping.

"Doc, this ain't worth your time," the voice said.

Doc's face relaxed into a smile. He picked up his whiskey and drank it.

"Why don't you go on with Johnny," the voice said. Behan knew it was an Earp, though he wasn't sure which one; they all sounded the same.

"I'll get a couple of boys," the voice said, "and go down to Wells Spicer's office and post bond."

"I was thinking I might shoot this pismire," Holliday said.

"Watch that ten-gauge, Billy," the voice said, and a man stepped past Behan and took Holliday's gun from its holster. Behan still didn't know which Earp it was until he turned, holding Doc's gun, and it was Wyatt. Wyatt stuck the gun in his belt.

"Come on, Doc," Wyatt said. "I'll walk down with you."

Holliday fell into step beside Wyatt, and the two of them walked through the ring of deputies and toward the saloon door.

"I'll be seeing you, bitch," Holliday said to Kate Elder as they passed her.

Behan had nothing to do but follow. And the deputies strung out behind him as they went out onto Allen Street and headed for the jail.

Thirty-two

Doc was out on bail within the hour, and in three days the county attorney dropped all charges.

"Said he couldn't find no grounds for them, Wyatt," Doc said, sipping whiskey and beer at the bar of the Alhambra. "I'm going to slap that bitch silly."

"Maybe you didn't hit her so much," Wyatt said, "she might not say bad things about you."

"They got her drunk," Doc said. "Behan and his crowd. Filled her with hooch and got her to sign the complaint. She's drunk, she'd sign a complaint against Jesus Christ."

"Specially if he thumped her around," Wyatt said. Doc laughed.

"Well, she's gone off to Globe for a while, waiting for me to cool down, I suppose."

Wyatt was drinking coffee, even though the temperature in the street was over a hundred.

"How come you never have a drink, Wyatt?"

"Don't like it."

"What don't you like?"

"Don't like the taste. Don't like being dull and slow and loud from drinking it."

"Like me?"

"Ain't seen you dull and slow yet, but you do get loud."

Doc finished his whiskey and ordered more.

"I do," Doc said. "That's a fact. You know why I drink so much, Wyatt?"

"Yeah," Wyatt said, "I do."

"Being a drunk and having a temper like I do might get me killed someday."

"Might."

"You know I don't care if it happens," Doc said.

"I know."

Doc drank some more whiskey and tipped his head back, letting the whiskey trickle down his throat. Then he swallowed and laughed and chased it with some beer.

"And I like whiskey, and beer, and," he laughed again, "and wild, wild women."

"Why do you suppose Behan put Kate up to that trick?" Wyatt said.

"You got his girl," Holliday said. "Johnny figured to paint me with shit and get some on you. You and Virgil ought to bring in them boys who really done the Benson stage. Take some of the bite out of Sheriff Behind."

"Got to locate them first," Wyatt said.

He wasn't looking at Holliday. He was gazing out through the saloon doors into the street.

"They're out there with the rustlers, Wyatt." Doc leaned back in his chair and made a wide sweeping gesture with his left hand. "Somewhere out there."

Wyatt smiled, still looking out the door.

"You ain't being much of a help, Doc."

"No, I probably ain't," Holliday said. "Mostly I'm probably a hindrance."

And he drank off the rest of his whiskey.

Thirty-three

The Citizens Safety Committee met in Schieffelin Hall two days after Pete Spence and Frank Stilwell had robbed the Bisbee Stage and been caught at once.

"Frank Stilwell's a goddamned deputy sheriff," Bill Herring said. "We can't trust the damned law officers; who we got left but ourselves?"

Milt Clapp tried to make a motion, but the noise in the room was too much. Everyone spoke at once. On one side of the room, Virgil leaned silently against the wall with Wyatt on one side and Morgan on the other. John Behan stood up beside Clapp and gestured for silence. No one paid him any mind. He waited. Several people yelled that everyone should shut up and let Johnny talk. The noise level dropped only slightly. But Behan jumped at it.

"You people are not fighting men," Behan said. "You can't go up against the cowboys."

The crowd roared that it damned well could, and was eager to do it.

"If you do this, at least get some people who know how to do it," Behan shouted. "You're a bank teller, Milton. Bill's a lawyer."

The crowd responded in a hundred tongues that it knew how to do it, and would be thrilled at the chance.

"The Earps are here," Behan shouted. "At least get some men like that with you. Let them be the enforcers."

The crowd liked the idea so much that it drowned any further sound that Behan might have made. The Earps were impassive against the wall.

"What's Johnny's game?" Morgan said.

"Putting us on the side of the vigilantes don't do us no good with the cowboys," Wyatt said.

"Hell, arresting Stilwell and Spence didn't do us all that much good," Virgil said.

"Frank McLaury's tight with both of them," Morgan said. "Him and the Clantons. They'll be cussing us out for sure."

"Give me the real rustlers anytime," Wyatt said.

"Like Ringo?" Morgan said.

Wyatt nodded.

"And Curley Bill," Wyatt said. "Those boys make their run, and if the law catches them at it, they expect the law to arrest them. They don't take it like you insulted them."

The crowd, having roared its approval of the Earps, was now roaring its disapproval of murder and robbery and ignoring the Earps entirely. There was a good deal of movement on the floor, and the Safety Committee members were jostling each other unmercifully.

"Remember we took Bill in after he shot Fred White?" Virgil said.

"That's what I mean," Wyatt said. "He knew we had to."

"Bill's a stand-up fella," Virgil said. "John Ringo too, when he's sober. Shame they get lumped in with people like Clanton and McLaury."

The Citizens Safety Committee was now making so much noise that the Earps could barely hear their own conversation.

"Let's get out of here," Morgan said.

When they left, no one except Behan noticed that they'd gone.

Thirty-four

They lay on their bed at the Cosmopolitan, with the window open so that the wind that drifted up from the west end of Allen Street played across their naked bodies.

"Your brothers like me, Wyatt?"

"Yes."

"How come we never spend time with them together?"

"Trouble with the women," Wyatt said. " 'Specially Allie."

"Virgil's wife?"

"Uh-huh."

"She close to Mattie?"

"Lot closer now than she was when I lived with Mattie," Wyatt said.

"You run into Johnny at all?"

"Now and then," Wyatt said.

"He don't give you any trouble, does he?"

"Not straight on he don't," Wyatt said.

"Straight on isn't Johnny's way," Josie said.

She propped herself on her left elbow and ran her right hand lightly over Wyatt's chest and stomach, tracing the muscles of his abdomen with the tips of her fingers.

"He's awful tight with the cowboys," she said.

"I know."

"What's wrong between you and the cowboys, Wyatt? I know there's hard feeling, but I don't know why."

"Not just me," Wyatt said. "All the Earps."

"Why? What have you done to them?"

"Not much. We fronted the McLaury boys once over some mules. Doc got into it with Ike Clanton."

"But Doc's not you."

"He's with us," Wyatt said.

"Why?" Josie said.

"He was with us in Dodge," Wyatt said.

"That's no answer," Josie said.

"Best answer I got."

"You know Doc's nothing but trouble. He's drunk most of the time. He's crazy when he's drunk."

"Hell, Josie, Doc's crazy when he's sober," Wyatt said.

"So why is he with you?"

"Because he is. This isn't San Francisco. It's hard living out here, and you don't always get to pick the people that'll side with you. Sometimes they pick you."

"Like Doc."

"Doc would walk into the barrel of a cannon with me," Wyatt said.

Josie was quiet. Wyatt raised on an elbow and looked at her. Her skin was very white. It was still hot in the desert, and her body was damp with perspiration. Wyatt bent over and kissed her gently on the mouth. She smiled at him.

"I don't mean to be full of questions," she said.

"You can ask me anything you wish," Wyatt said.

"It's complicated being a man," Josie said.

"It's easy enough," Wyatt said, "knowing what to do. It's hard sometimes to do it."

"I don't think it's so hard for you."

"Hard for everybody, Josie." He smiled and kissed her again. "Even us."

"I think even *knowing* what he should do was hard for Johnny."

"He sure as hell doesn't know what he shouldn't do," Wyatt said.

"I don't think Johnny is a bad man," Josie said. "He's more a bad combination of weak and ambitious, I think."

"Doesn't finally matter which it is," Wyatt said. "Comes to the same thing. It can get him killed."

He could see the softness go out of Josie's naked body.

"No," she said.

"No?"

"Not by you, Wyatt."

"I didn't say it would be me."

"It can't be you. I can't be in your bed knowing you killed the man I used to sleep with."

"Josie, we both know he wasn't the first."

"Doesn't matter," she said. "I couldn't."

"And if he came at me?"

"He won't," Josie said.

"You know that."

"He's afraid of you, Wyatt."

"But if he did," Wyatt said.

"That would be different," Josie said. "I'd rather you kill him than he kill you."

"Good."

"But only to save your life," Josie said. "You have to promise."

"Josie, I can't know what will happen. Virgil being city marshal is making Johnny look bad. He doesn't want any Earps running against him for sheriff. He's embarrassed that Morgan knocked him on his ass. And there's you and me."

"He won't try you, Wyatt."

"Maybe not head-on," Wyatt said. "But he's got most of the cowboys turned against us. I think he'll try to use Curley Bill and Ringo."

Josie turned and pressed the full length of her nakedness against him.

With her mouth pressed hard against him she said, "Promise. Promise."

He held her against him and kissed her back.

"Promise," she said fiercely. "Promise."

"Yes," he whispered. "I promise."

He felt her hands pressed against his back, her finger-nails digging into him. He held her damp body, with all his force, against him. She groaned, and softened, and neither of them whispered again.

Thirty-five

Virgil Earp was standing in the street outside the Grand Hotel, his back against one of the posts that held up the porch, one heel hooked over the edge of the boardwalk. It was mid-September and the soft desert fall had finally broken the summer heat. Two women wearing eastern clothes came out of the hotel and paused behind Virgil.

One of them said, "What of the Apaches, Marshal?"

Virgil took off his hat and turned toward the women.

"Haven't seen none in Tombstone, ma'am," Virgil said.

"We heard that General Carr's men were slaughtered and that the Apaches are coming this way."

Virgil smiled. Every time some buck killed a wood hauler the fear of Indian attack raged through Tombstone like dysentery.

"I don't think so, ma'am. They had a little skirmish, I think. Apaches normally head for Mexico when the Army's after them. They might pass by here, but they got no good reason to slow themselves down by riding into town."

"Wasn't there a meeting at Schieffelin Hall last night?"

"There's a lot of meetings in Tombstone, ma'am. It's about as meeting a town as I know," Virgil said. "No need to worry about the White Mountain Apaches. They got enough troubles without adding in Tombstone."

The two women hesitated and then moved on as Frank McLaury turned the corner from Fourth Street and stopped next to Virgil.

"Frank," Virgil said. His voice was easy as it always was, as if he had few problems and all the time in the world.

"I understand that you're raising up a vigilance committee to hang us boys," McLaury said.

"You boys?"

"You know," McLaury said, "us, the Clantons, Ringo, all the cowboys."

"Remember the time Curley Bill killed White?" Virgil said.

"Everybody does."

"Who guarded him that night," Virgil said, "and run him up to Tucson in the morning, so's to keep the Vigilance Committee from hangin' him?"

"I guess it was you boys," McLaury said.

He was staring down at the dirt of Allen Street.

"So maybe we don't altogether belong to the Vigilance Committee," Virgil said.

McLaury shook his head, looking at the street.

"You believe we do?" Virgil said.

"I got to believe the man told me that you do," McLaury said.

"Who told you that we do?"

"Johnny," McLaury said.

"Johnny Behan?"

"Yes."

"You don't have to believe Johnny Behan about much," Virgil said.

"He's always been straight with us boys," McLaury said.

"He's not straight this time, Frank."

"You and your brothers come for us, there'll be shooting. I don't intend to strangle on a rope."

McLaury turned sharply and walked away without looking back, as if he had frightened himself a little by what he'd said. Virgil looked after him until McLaury turned into the Oriental a block up and on the other side of Allen Street.

Thirty-six

It was October and Tombstone weather was finally comfortable. Wyatt was having breakfast with Josie in Maison Dorée, next to the Cosmopolitan Hotel.

"You ever see any Indians?" Josie said.

Wyatt smiled.

"No," he said. "Got a chance to eat breakfast, though, with the McLaurys and Curley Bill."

"My God," Josie said. "Really?"

"Yep. Weather got too bad to chase Indians in, rained so hard the horses were sinking into the mud half a foot. So we gave it up and headed back in. Stopped at Frink's place for a bit to get out of the weather and then the whole posse went on to McLaury's for breakfast. Fed us good, too."

"But aren't they your enemies?"

Wyatt smiled and put a piece of bacon in his mouth.

"Not when I was eating their food," Wyatt said.

"Not even Curley Bill?"

"Me and him didn't talk," Wyatt said. "But Virgil and him did. Seemed to be getting along fine."

"What did they talk about?"

"Don't know."

"And you didn't ask afterwards?"

"Nope."

"Don't you men talk?" Josie said.

She ate so pretty, he thought. She had a bowl of canned peaches. She cut off a bite-sized portion of one peach half and put it in her mouth with a fork, and chewed carefully with her mouth closed.

"We talk," Wyatt said.

"So what about the Indians?"

"Army's chasing them now."

"Will they catch them?"

Wyatt smiled widely.

"The Army?" he said.

"Yes."

"Army's mostly kids from Chicago and Boston," Wyatt said. "They can't catch their own mounts in the morning. Their officers been shipped out here for failing someplace else. Pretty much they're just putting in time until retirement." Wyatt shook his head and smiled again. "The Army couldn't catch Naitche if he was drinking agency whiskey at Fort Apache."

"You didn't catch him either," Josie said.

"No," Wyatt said, "we didn't."

Thirty-seven

It was after midnight when Wyatt sat down at the counter of the Occidental Lunch Room off the main room of the Alhambra Saloon. He ordered beefsteak and stewed tomatoes and drank some coffee while he waited for the meal. In the Alhambra, the bar was crowded, the faro tables were full and the sound of glasses and drunken men was loud. Ike Clanton came in from the saloon and sat down at the far end of the counter. He nodded at Wyatt, who nodded back, gave his order to the counter man and looked around the half-empty Lunch Room.

Wyatt's dinner was on the counter before him, and he was finishing the first cup of coffee when Doc Holliday came in. He had the high flush along the line of his cheekbones that he always got when he was drinking or when his lungs were acting up. His dark eyes seemed to recess deeper into his thin face when he drank. He was wearing a black cloth coat over a white shirt. The coat hung open.

"Clanton, you lying sonova bitch," Doc said.

"You got no call to be talking to me like that, Doc."

"You been telling people that Wyatt Earp blabbed to me about your and his plans."

"Doc, you're drunk," Clanton said. "I don't know what the hell you're talking about."

Doc's hand eased up to the edge of his coat, resting against his chest.

"You sonova bitch cowboy, you calling me drunk?" he said. "You go for your goddamned gun, and we'll see how drunk I am."

"I ain't heeled," Clanton said.

Wyatt got up and walked to the doorway that separated the saloon from the Lunch Room. Morgan was in the saloon, doing special deputy duty, keeping order. He saw Wyatt in the doorway. Wyatt jerked his head, and Morgan strolled past the faro players and into the Lunch Room.

"You ain't heeled?" Doc's rage spiraled and he could barely talk. He sounded, Wyatt thought, as if he were spitting.

"You sonova bitch," Holliday said, "go heel yourself, you ain't heeled."

Morgan walked past Doc and hoisted his backside up and sat on the counter between Doc and Clanton and let his heels dangle. Morgan's coat hung open, and the butt of his big Colt showed. He rested his hand against his body near the gun.

"I ain't afraid of you, Holliday, even if all the Earps in Tombstone are backing you up."

"I ain't exactly backed Doc here," Morgan said, "but you sonova bitch, you keep talking and you are going to have all the fight you want right now."

Wyatt went back to his end of the counter and began to eat. Virgil came into the Lunch Room from the street and stood in the doorway. He had a deputy with him named Jim Flynn.

"Take Doc out of here, Morg," Virgil said.

"Nobody takes Doc out of anywhere," Holliday said.

Morgan grinned at him and swung down from the lunch counter and stood beside Holliday. He was probably a foot taller than Doc.

"Come on, John Henry," Morgan said.

He put his hand on Holliday's arm and turned him slightly toward the door and walked him past Virgil and out into the street. Clanton looked down the counter at Wyatt for a moment, then he turned and went out the same door that Morgan and Doc had gone through into the street. Wyatt continued to eat his steak and tomatoes. The tomatoes had some green chilies cut up in them and had been heated with several squares of bread tossed in. As he ate, he could hear Doc's spitting rage outside and Ike Clanton's voice almost as frantic and just as angry. Wyatt gestured with his cup to the counterman and the counterman came down and poured him more coffee. As he drank some of the fresh coffee, blowing on it first so as not to burn his lip, he heard Virgil's voice in the street.

"Goddamm it, that's enough," Virgil said. "Either you go in different directions, or I'll arrest both of you right now."

Wyatt stood and walked to the door. In the street Doc was walking away. Morgan walked beside him, herding him with his bulk. Ike lingered for a moment, looking at Virgil, looking over his shoulder at Wyatt. Then he turned and walked past Virgil in the other direction.

"Don't you bastards shoot me in the back," Ike said.

Virgil watched him go, then nodded at Wyatt and walked off down Allen Street.

Wyatt went back to the counter and finished his meal. Then at about 1:30 in the morning Wyatt left the Occidental and strolled up Allen Street toward the Crystal Palace to pick up the bank money from his faro game. Ike Clanton was in the street, with a Colt revolver in his belt.

"Wyatt," Clanton said.

"Ike."

"I just want you to know that I ain't a man to walk away from a fight."

Wyatt didn't say anything.

"I wasn't fixed just right when Doc fronted me in there," Clanton said.

Again Wyatt was silent. He began to move along the street toward the Crystal Palace.

"In the morning I'm going up against Doc, man to man. All this fighting talk has gone on long enough."

"You know how Doc blows off," Wyatt said. "He just wanted you to know I didn't tell any secrets."

"Like hell," Ike said. "And don't think I won't fight you too. All of you. I'll be ready for all of you in the morning."

"I don't see any reason to fight somebody if I can get away from it," Wyatt said. "There's no money in it."

"You better be ready tomorrow," Ike said. "Doc and you and your brothers."

"Try to get some sleep, Ike," Wyatt said and turned into the Crystal Palace.

Thirty-eight

They played poker all night. Virgil Earp, Johnny Behan, Ike Clanton, Tom McLaury, and another man none of them knew. Mostly it was five-card draw, and by morning Virgil had won some money. With the sun shining down Allen Street and throwing long shadows in front of it, Virgil stuffed his revolver into his belt and stepped into the street with Ike behind him.

"I don't see why you have to play cards all night with a Colt in your lap," Ike said.

"I'm a peace officer," Virgil said. "I like to keep it handy."

"Well, it ain't comforting, being as you was throwing in with them that want to murder me."

"I'm throwing in with the law," Virgil said.

"Well, you want to have at me, I'm in town."

"I been up all night, Ike," Virgil said. "I'm going home and go to bed."

"Well, 'fore you do that, I want you to carry a message to Doc Holliday," Ike said. "The son of a bitch has got to fight me."

"That's no way to talk to a peace officer. I want you to be easy while I'm sleeping."

"You won't carry the message?" Ike said.

" 'Course I won't."

"Well, he'll have to fight, damn his ass. You may have to fight too, 'fore you know it."

Virgil shrugged and turned west on Allen Street with the sun behind him and his shadow ten feet long in the empty dirt street. At home, Allie was awake but not yet up. She watched as he undressed and put the big Colt on the bedside table before he climbed in.

"There something going on?" she said.

"Been trying to keep Doc and Ike Clanton from killing each other," Virgil said.

"Why didn't you let them go ahead?" Allie said. "Neither one of them amounts to snake spit."

Virgil patted her hip as she lay on her side beside him.

"Doc's been with us a long time," Virgil said, and fell asleep almost at once with his hand resting on her hip.

Allie lay on her side for a while looking at him. There was in him such a great calmness that he could fall asleep like that. He was motionless as he slept. His breathing was even. After a while she gently took his hand away from her hip and laid it on the blanket and got up and began to make herself some breakfast. At midmorning she came into the bedroom. Virgil came wide awake as she opened the door. He was always like that, she thought. Either full asleep or full awake. He never seemed in between.

"Bronk's here," she said. "Got jail business. Something about a prisoner."

"Tell him I'll be in later this afternoon," Virgil said.

"Bronk also says that you better get up because Ike Clanton is on a rampage and there's liable to be hell. Says Ike's threatening to kill Doc, and you boys too."

Virgil nodded.

"Ike's probably drunk," Virgil said. "Tell Bronk I'll be in later this afternoon."

He closed his eyes and appeared to be instantly asleep. Allie went out to tell Bronk what Virgil had said. When he left she picked up where she'd left off ironing Virgil's shirts. While she let the iron heat on the stove she thought about Ike Clanton. He was a mean, loudmouthed drunk. She knew that. She'd seen a lot like him in saloons in Wichita and Dodge and Ellsworth. And she knew that mean, loudmouthed drunks with a gun could be dangerous. He'd need to be drunk to go up against Virgil; the whiskey would give him fortitude. But it didn't mean he couldn't pull the trigger. She thought about going to Virgil's brothers. She knew they'd stand with him. It was who Bronk had meant when he said Clanton would be going after "you boys." The Earps were always "you boys," she thought. She took the iron off the stove with a potholder and licked her finger and tapped it on the flat of the iron. It sizzled. She nodded and began to iron careful creases in the shirt she'd stretched out on the board. Always "you boys." Always the brothers. It was a good thing sometimes. Sometimes it was bad. She set the iron on its heel and turned the shirt and ironed another careful crease. She decided not to go to Wyatt or Morgan. Virgil wouldn't approve. And God knew he'd handled things like this before. He slept peacefully in the next room while a man raged in the streets threatening to kill him. Maybe Ike would call Doc out before Virgil even woke up, and Doc would kill Ike, and it would be past. Allie took a deep breath and let it out slowly and kept ironing.

Thirty-nine

Just before noon Katie Elder was looking at some of Camillus Fly's photographs in the gallery Fly kept next to his rooming house. Fly came in.

"Ike Clanton's out there with a rifle and a side arm," Fly said. "He is looking for Mr. Holliday."

"Why?" Kate said.

"He says he is going to kill him," Fly said.

"Doc'll be interested to hear that," Kate said.

She went next door into the boardinghouse and up to their room and woke Doc up.

"Ike Clanton's looking to kill you," Kate said. "He's got a rifle."

Doc rolled out of bed and began to put on his pants.

" 'Less I die on the way," Doc said, "he'll get his chance."

The air smelled of impending snow when Wyatt met Virgil and Morgan on Fremont Street. It was cold for October. All three men wore mackinaws; the hem of Wyatt's was tucked up above the walnut handle of his gun.

"Harry Jones tells me Ike is after us with a Winchester and a six-shooter," Wyatt said.

Virgil nodded.

"He was down at Hafford's, too," Morgan said, "with a rifle. Says he was insulted last night when he wasn't fixed right. Says he's heeled now and ready and wants to fight."

"Lynch told me the same thing," Virgil said. "Says Ike's planning to kill us on sight."

"And the sonova bitch been telling people we was supposed to meet him at noon and welshed out on it," Morgan said. "It ain't even noon yet."

"Five of," Wyatt said.

"Seems to me," Virgil said, "we ought to find him and settle him down a bit."

"Maybe we should settle him down for good," Morgan said. "Ike's starting to make me awful tired."

"We'll disarm him, arrest him if we can," Virgil said.

"I'll go up to Allen Street," Wyatt said. "See if I can find him, see what he wants."

Morgan and Virgil began to look for Ike along Fremont. Wyatt walked up Fourth Street toward Allen. He could smell snow in the air. He shrugged himself a little deeper inside the mackinaw and put his hands into his coat pockets. Wouldn't want them stiff with cold if he was going to have to shoot Ike Clanton.

Behind him Ike came out of the Capitol Saloon. He looked toward Wyatt. Virgil, with Morgan beside him, came around the corner of Fremont and took hold of Ike's rifle barrel with his left hand. Wyatt turned.

Virgil said, "Are you hunting for me?"

"I am, goddamn you, and if I seen you a second sooner you'd be dead."

Wyatt began to walk back toward them. Ike went for the six-shooter he wore stuck into his waistband. Virgil hit Ike on the side of his head with the big Colt revolver he was carrying. Ike grunted and sank to his knees. He stayed down for a moment, shaking his head, and then looked up into the barrel of Morgan's six-shooter. Ike could see that it was cocked.

"We're arresting you, Ike, for carrying a concealed weapon," Virgil said.

Wyatt was there now, standing beside Morgan. Virgil reached down and took Ike's revolver and handed both guns to Morgan.

"You fucking Earps don't give a man a chance," Ike said.

"We didn't shoot you," Virgil said.

Forty

Recorder's Court was across the street in one of Dick Gird's block of buildings. Ike sat on one of the benches holding a handkerchief against the oozing cut on his head.

"I'm going to go find Judge Wallace," Virgil said.

Morgan leaned against the wall holding Ike's weapons. Wyatt sat on the bench next to Ike, turned so he could face him. The courtroom was crowded, and everyone in it stared at them.

"I'll get even for this," Ike said. "I had something to shoot with, I'd fight you all right now."

Morgan smiled and held out a Henry Rifle, muzzle down. Ike stared at it. People around them in the courtroom scattered into the street.

"I'll tell you what, Ike," Morgan said. "I'll pay your damn fine if you'll fight us."

Ike didn't move.

"You thieving sonova bitch," Wyatt said. "You've been threatening our lives, and you know it. I could shoot you right here and be justified."

"Fight is my racket," Ike said. "All I want is four feet of ground."

Morgan continued to hold out the rifle. Ike continued not to take it.

"Okay, how about a six-gun too," Morgan said and offered Ike the Colt he'd taken from him earlier.

Ike didn't move. One of Behan's deputies, a squat muscular man whom Wyatt didn't know, stepped in front of Ike.

"No fuss now," the deputy said, "I don't want any fuss."

Judge Wallace entered the room in back and walked toward the front. There was a big cast-iron stove near the bench. The judge took off his overcoat and hung it on a hook behind his bench. Then he sat down and looked at Clanton and the Earps. The onlookers, who had scattered when the rifle was offered, trailed back in behind the judge. The people close to the stove took off their coats. It was too hot to wear them on the side that faced the stove, though it was cold without a coat on the side away from the stove. The people farther from the stove kept their coats on.

"Nor do I want a fuss," he said. "What are the charges?"

"Apprehended Ike Clanton carried a concealed weapon on Fremont Street," Virgil said.

"Rather vigorously, I would say," Judge Wallace said, looking at Ike's bleeding head. "How do you plead?"

"Guilty, I guess . . . Your Honor."

Judge Wallace nodded.

"Twenty-five dollars."

Ike took money from his pocket and walked toward the judge with it. Wallace shook his head.

"Not me," he said, "give it to Mr. Campbell."

Ike looked embarrassed and veered to the clerk and handed him the money. The clerk wrote out a receipt and gave it to Ike.

"Next case," Judge Wallace said.

"Where you want to pick up your hardware, Ike?" Virgil said.

"Anyplace you won't be hitting my fucking head with your six-gun," Ike said and walked out of the room.

Virgil looked at Morgan and shrugged.

"Drop them off with the bartender," Virgil said, "over at the Grand."

Morgan left. Virgil stood with Wyatt in the courtroom, where the spectators still jostled one another and the cast-iron stove reeked unevenly of heat.

"This ain't gonna go away," Virgil said.

"No it ain't."

"Ike's a gasbag," Virgil said.

"It ain't just Ike," Wyatt said. "The McLaurys are wound up too, and you know that it's Behan did the winding."

"Which means probably that Brocius will be in," Virgil said.

"And Johnny Ringo."

"Too bad," Virgil said.

"Yes, I like him too."

"Maybe I should settle this with Behan," Wyatt said.

"Behan won't fight you," Virgil said. "He's got Ike and the cowboys to do that."

Wyatt didn't say anything.

"Besides which, he's the goddamned sheriff," Virgil said.

Still, Wyatt was silent, watching the business of the courtroom slowly proceed.

"Maybe," Wyatt said, "we ought to get to it instead of waiting around for one of them to back-shoot us."

"I'm the city marshal, Wyatt."

"I'm not," Wyatt said.

"You shoot somebody down in the street," Virgil said, "I'm going to have trouble covering that."

"My guess is, they ain't going to give us a choice."

"If they don't," Virgil said, "they don't. We'll play the cards that turn up."

Forty-one

Wyatt was glad to be outside. After the stove-tainted courthouse he liked the cold air, the smell of impending snow. The feel of a storm approaching was about right. He walked up Fourth Street, nodding to Bauer the butcher and another man whose name he did not know. Coming toward him from the corner of Allen was Tom McLaury. McLaury slowed for a moment as if he might turn and go another way. Then he seemed to right himself, and continued toward Wyatt. McLaury had the thumb of his right hand hooked into his belt.

"What have you boys done to Ike Clanton?" Tom said.

"Run him in for carrying a concealed weapon," Wyatt said. "He whistle for you and your brother?"

"I got a right to be in town," McLaury said.

"And I got a right to ask what you're doing here."

Wyatt could feel the cold fire at the center of himself. It sharpened everything for him as it always did. Every pore in McLaury's face seemed discrete and obvious, his eyelashes individuated.

Wyatt could smell things sharply and hear things clearly. He was focused microscopically and yet intensely aware of things at the very faint periphery of his vision. He felt solid and quick.

"You got no reason to talk to me like that, Wyatt. I'm a friend of yours."

"Not if you're a friend of Ike's," Wyatt said. "You here backing Ike?"

"I never done nothing against you boys," McLaury said. "But if you're looking for a fight, I'll fight."

"You heeled?" Wyatt said.

"Maybe I am," McLaury said.

"Then jerk your gun," Wyatt said.

With his left hand he slapped McLaury across the face. With his right he pulled the big smooth-handled Colt that he'd once used to face down Clay Allison. McLaury staggered back from the slap, his right hand still fumbling at his belt. Wyatt slammed him across the face with the four-pound revolver and McLaury went down and stayed. Wyatt looked down at him for a moment, then stepped past him carefully and walked on toward Hafford's Saloon at the corner of Allen Street.

Wyatt bought a cigar at Hafford's, and got it lit and burning evenly before he went back outside and stood on the boardwalk in front of the saloon. He was halfway through the cigar when Frank McLaury rode up Allen

Street on the other side with Billy Clanton and Major Frink. They dismounted, tied their horses and went into the Grand Hotel.

The smell of snow was strong. Wyatt took the cigar from his mouth and examined the glowing tip of it, turning it slightly to see that it was burning evenly. Then he put the cigar back in his mouth and leaned his back against the wall of Hafford's and waited.

The cigar was an inch shorter when Frank McLaury and Billy Clanton came out of the Grand Hotel, crossed Allen, trailing their horses behind them, and headed down Fourth Street. If they saw Wyatt standing outside of Hafford's, they gave no sign.

Wyatt watched them as they went and then tossed the cigar into the street and stepped off behind them. He felt strong and compact. His muscles felt easy. His breathing was easy. The cold desert air filled his lungs. Halfway down Fourth Street, there was a crowd of people outside of Spangenberg's Gun Shop, maybe a dozen, maybe more. Frank and Billy pushed through the crowd and went in. Wyatt drifted along toward the crowd and several people moved out of his way when he got close. Frank McLaury's whitestockinged bay horse was on the sidewalk with his head in the door of the gun shop. Past the horse, inside Spangenberg's, Wyatt could see Ike Clanton, his head still bleeding, Tom McLaury, Billy Clanton and Frank McLaury. Wyatt took his hat off with his left hand and shooed the horse off the sidewalk and into the street. While he did it he kept his eyes on Spangenberg's door. The four cowboys appeared in the doorway. Billy Clanton had his hand on his gun.

"I'll take my horse," Frank McLaury said, and took hold of the reins with his left hand.

"You'll have to keep him off the sidewalk," Wyatt said. McLaury and he looked at each other.

"Watch toward Allen Street, Frank," Tom McLaury said.

Virgil Earp had rounded the corner of Allen and Fourth, his hat pulled low against the cold, carrying a ten-gauge shotgun. He walked slowly toward them and leaned on the wall of a doorway across the street.

"Bob Hatch said you was down here, Wyatt."

"Just clearing this horse off the sidewalk," Wyatt said.

"Town ordinance," Virgil said. "No horses on the sidewalk."

Frank backed the horse off the sidewalk and into the street and wrapped the reins around the hitching rail in front of Spangenberg's. Wyatt stood quietly watching. Virgil stayed where he was in the doorway, the shotgun over his forearm, the double-barrels aimed loosely toward the cowboys. Most of the dozen or so people who had crowded around to see what was going on when Ike had stumbled in there with his head bleeding, had backed away out of any line of fire that might develop. The McLaurys went back into the gun shop. Wyatt could see Billy Clanton feeding shells into his cartridge belt from a box that Frank McLaury was holding. Wyatt turned and walked past McLaury's horse, across Fourth Street, and joined his brother in the doorway.

"Guess you're still covered by that temporary marshal appointment," Virgil said.

"Guess so," Wyatt said.

"Seen you let crimes like that pass, though," Virgil said.

"Horse on the sidewalk. It's unlawful, unsanitary, and dangerous to the citizenry," Wyatt said. "Damned horse coulda stepped on somebody's foot."

"You're pushing this kind of hard," Virgil said, still staring across the street at the gun shop.

The wind had picked up, and both men were glad to be sheltered in the doorway. An occasional spat of snow drifted in on the wind.

"It's going to happen, Virgil. Might as well move it along."

"Might not happen."

"It'll happen," Wyatt said.

"You want it to happen," Virgil said.

"Hell, it's about me and Josie," Wyatt said. "We both know that."

"Maybe. But you think Ike knows it, or the McLaurys?"

"Nope. But Behan knows it."

Ike Clanton came out of the gun shop with his brother,

and Billy Claiborne and the McLaurys, and walked silently past, without a glance at the Earps, toward Allen Street.

"Might make less of a mess," Virgil said as his eyes followed the cowboys, "if you and Johnny settled it between you."

"He won't go against me straight out," Wyatt said.

"No," Virgil said. "He won't."

"So he stirs up the cowboys and hopes they'll do it for them."

"He think you'll be alone?" Virgil said. "He think you don't have brothers?"

Wyatt looked out of the doorway at Fourth Street. Now and then an isolated snowflake drifted past.

"How about Doc?" Virgil said.

"Doc will be with us if he feels like fighting."

"If he hasn't got a hangover," Virgil said.

"Or maybe if he has," Wyatt said.

"If there's a fight."

"There'll be a fight," Wyatt said.

"You want it to come?" Virgil said.

"Time to lance this boil," Wyatt said.

"More than that," Virgil said.

"Maybe."

Forty-two

Morgan came out of Hafford's Saloon and joined his brothers and Doc Holliday in front of Hafford's, on the corner of Fourth and Allen. The Doc was wearing a long gray coat and carrying a cane.

"Heard we was going to shoot some cowboys," Doc said.

Virgil nodded. "Might have to," he said.

"Care to join us?" Morgan said.

Doc took a nickel-plated revolver from his right-hand coat pocket and pretended to shoot it twice, making soft puffing sounds to indicate the shots.

"Don't mind if I do," Doc said. "You ready, Wyatt?"

Wyatt nodded. He felt himself steadily clarifying, as if some sort of internal telescope were slowly coming into focus. He had the big Colt Peacemaker in his belt. It seemed to be just right there, as if when he took hold of it it became him, part of his hand, an extension of his reach. His collar was turned up, and he felt warm and steady inside the wool mackinaw. He could feel the strength in his muscles. His heartbeat was steady. His legs felt springy. His hands felt soft and comfortable. There were people coming out of Hafford's, and going into Hafford's, and walking past on both Allen and Fourth Streets. But they seemed now insubstantial, not invisible, but immaterial as he leaned his back against the wall of the saloon again and waited. It would come; it was like an empty railroad car that had been started on a downgrade, moving persistently faster, becoming always more inevitable. One had only to wait its arrival at the bottom of the grade. Except for the weather, it was the way he'd felt when he faced down Clay Allison in Dodge.

"Where are they?" Doc said.

"Dexter's Corral," Virgil answered. "Look."

The cowboys came out of Dexter's and crossed the street and entered the O.K. Corral. As they disappeared into the livery area, J. L. Phonic walked up Fourth Street and stopped in front of Virgil. The collar of his long black coat was turned up against the wind. His smallish townsman's hat was pulled down hard on his head.

"You need them, I can deliver ten men with Winchesters right now," Phonic said.

"Don't expect to need them," Virgil said. "Those boys stay in the O.K. Corral, we won't bother them."

"Why those boys down on Fremont Street right now, near your rooming house, Doc?"

"Looking for me, probably," Doc said.

"They're heeled," Virgil said.

"Sure," Phonic said.

"Well, I guess we better go down there and disarm them," Virgil said.

He handed the shotgun to Doc.

"Keep that under your coat, Doc. Don't want people getting the wrong idea and going off too quick."

Doc gave his cane to Virgil and stowed the shotgun, holding it inside his coat with his left hand.

"Here we go," Virgil said.

Things at large were going very fast now, but the small details were getting steadily slower. Everything Wyatt looked at seemed leisurely and somehow stately. The wind had stopped. The movement of his brothers and Doc as they began the walk down Fourth Street was timeless and made no sound. Johnny Behan appeared and spoke to them and was brushed aside. A two-horse hitch moved past them going silently in the opposite direction, moving as if it had wound down, the big draft horses nearly balletic in their slow elegance. He could feel the steady rhythm of his pulse, the easy flow of his blood. There was nothing on the periphery anymore. The buildings along Fourth Street disappeared as he walked, and he felt Virgil and Morgan and Doc to his left. They walked abreast, Wyatt on the far right. He knew there was coldness and the smell of snow. Now and then a random and singular snowflake would drift in front of him. He felt the weight of the six-shooter in his belt. Everything seemed to be happening soundlessly at the bottom of a clear lake. They were at Fremont Street. It had taken no time at all, and yet it had moved more slowly than it seemed possible to move. Wyatt didn't want it hurried. If Josie were with him here in this crystalline moment there could be no heaven to match it. As it was, he felt as if his life had compacted into a density that no harm could penetrate. He opened his hands wide and let them relax and stretched them again for the sheer physical surge of it. Everything was profoundly intense, nearly magical. Ike was there with Billy Clanton and the McLaurys, clustered in the alley together beside Fly's. Virgil's voice came from beyond a vast emptiness. Something about "Throw up your hands . . ." and then, "Hold on, I don't mean that . . ." and then gunfire. His big Army Colt ahead of him, an extension of himself, the hammer thumbed back, bucking slightly as the hammer fell. Around him, barely penetrating his focus, other guns were firing as if at a great distance. Frank is hit, and Billy Clanton, and his brother Morgan. Ike closes with him for a moment. Wyatt tosses him aside. Ike runs. Tom shoots from behind his frightened horse. More shots. Hammer back. Pull the trigger. Again. The bullets seem to surge from his deepest self in a leisurely way. Doc staggers and curses and fires again. Clinging to his horse, firing over him, Frank takes a few steps into Third Street and falls. The horse shies off, his reins trailing, and trots down Third Street. Tom is down in the alley. Billy Clanton is on the ground, his back against the wall of Fly's, still cocking and firing. Another shot. Billy slumps. Then vast silence. As if time had stopped. Virgil was limping, a bullet through the calf. Morgan was in pain, a bullet in his shoulder. Billy Clanton was dead. Tom McLaury was dead. Frank was dead. In the utter stillness the smell of cordite was thick in the narrow alley. Wyatt still held the gun with its hammer back, moving the gun slowly before him back and forth, scanning the silence. Part of the silence, at one with it, as the occasional snowflake spiraled down, and the clean desert air that filled his lungs began to clarify the gun smoke.

Forty-three

Behan never looked quite comfortable, Wyatt thought, as the sheriff walked toward him. He was always a little too dressed up. When he wore a gun, it didn't hang quite right. On horseback he looked awkward, as if he'd be happier on foot. On foot, he looked as if he'd be easier sitting.

"I need to talk with you," Behan said, his voice distant, and surprising in the sulfurous quiet.

There was no one else to talk to but Wyatt. Ike had run. The McLaurys were dead, and Billy Clanton. Dr. Goodfellow was probing the wound in Virgil's calf. Morgan, in pain from his shoulder wound, was being loaded into a hack. Doc had retreated to Fly's boardinghouse with a bullet burn creasing his hip.

"I won't be arrested," Wyatt said. His own voice seemed to come from somewhere else.

"I'm the sheriff, Wyatt. I got to arrest you."

"If you were God, Johnny, I wouldn't let you arrest me. I'm not going away. I'll be around for the inquest."

"I warned you," Behan said.

"You fed us bullshit," Wyatt said. "You told us you'd disarmed them."

The hack with Morgan in it moved past them and Wyatt watched it as it went. The street was filled with people now, many of them men, many of them armed.

"I told you I *would* disarm them," Behan said.

Wyatt turned back from looking at the hack.

"Johnny," Wyatt said. "This is your fault. You couldn't come at me direct, so you rigged this."

"Wyatt, so help me, God . . ."

Wyatt shook his head.

"Don't talk to me now, Johnny. I can't talk to you. You got to get away from me."

Behan tried to hold Wyatt's eyes and couldn't and hesitated another moment and turned and walked away. Wyatt watched him go as he headed east on Fremont Street until he turned the corner by the post office at Fourth Street disappeared. He realized he was still holding his revolver. He could tell by the weight that it was empty. He opened the cylinder, ejected the shell casings, fished absently into his left-hand coat pocket and came out with a handful of fresh bullets. As he fed them one at a time into the cylinder, the coroner's people were gathering up the three dead men and loading them onto the back of a wagon. Wyatt snapped the cylinder shut and put the gun in his right-hand pocket. Another hack, carrying Virgil, moved slowly past him.

"They find the slug?" Wyatt asked.

"It went on through," Virgil said.

"Good," Wyatt said and the hack moved on.

Fremont Street in front of the alley was crowded now. To Wyatt the crowd was a phantasmagoria, as intangible as the projections of a magic lantern. It was what followed reality, trailing in the absolute fact of the gunfight, like the wisps of gun smoke that had already disappeared, dispersed by the fresh fall air. The coroner's wagon began to move away with the corpses of the McLaurys and Billy Clanton, and when it was gone Wyatt was the only embodiment of the facts that had transpired, alone in the insubstantial crowd of miners and cowboys that meaninglessly milled and chattered around him. People may have spoken to him. If they did he didn't hear them. He put the leftover shells back in his left-hand coat pocket, and put the newly loaded revolver in his right-hand coat pocket. Then he turned and went to find Josie.

Forty-four

They were in her room, sitting together on the bed. Josie's face was a white oval in the cold last light of the November day that came in through the window. A wood stove warmed the room.

"So it's over?" Josie said.

"Hearing's over," Wyatt said. "You want to hear what Spicer ruled?"

"Of course."

Wyatt's coat hung on a chair near the bed. He reached over and took paper from his inside coat pocket and unfolded it.

"*The evidence taken before me in this case,*" Wyatt read, "*would not, in my judgment, warrant a conviction of the defendants by a trial jury of any offense whatever.*"

"Of course, he's right," Josie said. "No one could have ruled differently."

Wyatt smiled a little. He put the paper back inside his coat.

"Maybe if Behan were running the hearing . . ." Wyatt said.

"Thank God he's not," she said.

Josie put her head against Wyatt's shoulder. He held her hand. They were quiet together in the still-moonlit room.

"Do you think Johnny put them up to it?" Josie said.

"Yes."

"Is it about me?" Josie said finally.

Wyatt thought about her question.

"It's about you and me," he said after a time. "There's been a lot of push and shove between us and the cowboys. And it'd be hard to get along with both sides. Johnny tried, but after you and me turned out to be what we are, it was pretty easy for him to slide over to the cowboys. I think he stirred them up, Ike especially, because Ike's pretty much a fool drunk and easy to stir up."

"Is he through trying?" Josie said.

"Not likely," Wyatt said.

"What do you think Johnny will do?" Josie said.

"He's got the rest of the cowboys to rile. Brocius, and John Ringo, for instance, are a little different than Ike and the McLaurys."

"Are you afraid of them?"

Wyatt shrugged.

"Thinking about that doesn't do me much good one way or the other," he said.

"And you have friends," Josie said.

"I do," Wyatt said and smiled. "And my brother Warren came in from California. He's planning to stay awhile."

"Is he like you?" Josie said.

"He's more like Morgan."

"Kind of likes trouble?" Josie said.

"Kind of."

"If only Johnny would just come out in the open," she said.

Wyatt shook his head.

"It's not Johnny's way," Wyatt said.

"I don't know what to wish," Josie said. "I can't wish that we hadn't met."

"No, you can't wish that," Wyatt said. "Whatever comes of all this, we are worth whatever it costs."

"Then I wish someone would kill Johnny."

"Someone would have to murder him," Wyatt said. "He won't come at you straight on."

"Could you murder him?"

"No."

"You've shot men before."

"It's not just what you do, it's how you do it," Wyatt said. "And I think I promised you I wouldn't."

"I know," Josie said. "I know."

"Shooting the sheriff is serious business. There's some law out here now. Hell, I'm supposed to be part of it sometimes."

"Maybe Doc," Josie said.

"That's up to Doc," Wyatt said. "I won't ask him to do my shooting for me. . . . And I don't want you asking him."

She rubbed her cheek against his shoulder.

"You know me quite well, don't you?" she said.

"I know you're talking different than you did when you made me promise not to shoot him."

"I didn't know it would get down to you or him."

"Things do," Wyatt said.

"And you knew they would."

"Yes."

"And you promised me anyway."

"I love you," Wyatt said.

"God, I'm such a little girl."

"You appear to me to be growing up fast," Wyatt said.

"What if I talked to Johnny?" Josie said.

"I don't like that, but even if I did, it don't really matter anymore. Thing like this has got a life all its own. The balls been opened. It'll run until it's done running."

"And we just wait for it to happen?"

"We can do a little better than that," Wyatt said. "We can be ready for it."

Forty-five

It was a Wednesday night, three days after Christmas. Wyatt and Virgil were at the bar in the Oriental. Virgil had a glass of beer. Wyatt was drinking coffee.

"Allie was wondering when Mattie was going to move into the hotel with the rest of us," Virgil said.

"Allie'll have to ask her direct," Wyatt said. "Mattie ain't got much to say to me."

"You ask her to come with you?" Virgil said.

"I told her she could."

"And she said no?"

"She didn't say anything," Wyatt said. "Mostly she just cries."

"Nobody'll bother her anyway," Virgil said.

"I know," Wyatt said.

"How about Josie?"

"Allie asking about her too?" Wyatt said.

"Nope, me."

"Hell, Virgil, this whole thing is about Behan wanting her back," Wyatt said. "He's not going to kill her?"

"Be a way to get at you," Virgil said.

"No, Johnny ain't much. But he won't hurt her."

"I agree he ain't much," Virgil said. "But since the fight and the trial he got a lot of people on his side now. And some of them are much."

"Curley Bill?"

"Yep, and John Ringo. Billy Breakenridge is a pretty good man. And Dave Neagle."

"And none of them would hurt Josie," Wyatt said.

"How 'bout Ike?" Virgil said. "Frank Stilwell? Pete Spence?"

Wyatt nodded.

"Okay. Maybe they would," he said.

"So whyn't you send her to San Francisco, let her father look after her, until we clean this up?"

Wyatt drank some of his coffee, holding it in both hands, looking over the rim through the ribbon of steam that rose from the cup. He put the cup down and grinned at Virgil.

" 'Cause she won't go," Wyatt said.

Virgil grinned back at him.

"I understand that," he said.

Virgil finished his beer.

"Well," he said, "time to go home."

"The Cosmopolitan Hotel is not home," Wyatt said.

"No, but the perimeter's a hell of a lot easier to secure."

"Home sweet home," Wyatt said.

Virgil said good night and turned and walked out of the front door of the Oriental.

Wyatt gestured at the bartender for more coffee, and

watched as it was poured. From the street came the sound of gunshots. Wyatt thought there were four. Shotguns, he was pretty sure. Two guns, both barrels? He turned toward the door as Virgil pushed into the saloon. The left side of him was bloody.

"I'm hurt, Wyatt," Virgil said.

He seemed calm enough, but Wyatt knew that the first shock of injury often left you calm. It hadn't yet started to hurt like it was going to.

"Where?" Wyatt said.

He stepped to his brother's side and put his left arm under Virgil's right arm and held him upright. Wyatt held a Colt .45 in his right hand, pointing at the floor with the hammer thumbed back.

"Empty building across the street," Virgil said.

"I meant, where are you hurt?"

"Left side, left arm," Virgil said.

"Can you walk to the hotel?"

"Yes."

Wyatt turned to Blonde Marie.

"Go across the street and get Goodfellow," Wyatt said. "We'll be at the Cosmopolitan."

Without a word Blonde Marie ran from the saloon.

They moved slowly out of the saloon, crossed Fifth Street, and walked almost the length of the block to the Cosmopolitan Hotel. It took them longer than it took the news. When they reached the hotel lobby Sherman McMasters was there, and Doc, and Morgan, all armed. Warren, slighter and darker than his brothers, was at the top of the stairs with a shotgun. Allie stood beside him. Her eyes were big, her face was white. When she saw them she clattered down the stairs.

"Bring him to our room," she said.

Dr. Goodfellow came into the lobby, and behind him Blonde Marie, who stopped awkwardly just inside the door to stare at the Earp women as they gathered around Virgil.

"Oh Virgil," Allie said, "oh goddammit, Virgil."

Virgil put his right arm around her.

"Still got one arm to hug you with, Allie."

Allie rested her head briefly against his shoulder and took in some air, and some of her briskness came back.

"Well, that'll be plenty," she said.

Wyatt and his brothers waited in the lobby while Goodfellow and a doctor named Matthews worked on Virgil. Blonde Marie in a burst of enthusiasm had sent one of the other whores to get Dr. Matthews, just to be on the safe side.

Doc was drinking in the lobby, walking back and forth with a whiskey glass and a bottle, swearing to himself, his black coat open and tucked on the right side behind the butt of his revolver. Sherman McMasters and Turkey Creek Jack Johnson were outside on the porch with shotguns. At two-fifteen in the morning, Dr. Goodfellow came down the stairs.

"Wound in his side is nothing," Goodfellow said. "But his left arm's a mess. We're going to have to take the elbow out."

"Will he be able to use it afterwards?" Wyatt said.

"Not much," Goodfellow said.

"He can still shoot," Wyatt said.

"A handgun," Goodfellow said and moved past Wyatt to take some medical supplies from George Parsons. Wyatt turned and looked at Morgan.

"You heard the doctor?" Wyatt said.

"Yes."

"Shots came from that construction on the corner," Wyatt said. "Get a lantern."

He and Morgan went out of the hotel and walked back up Allen Street, the lantern casting its uncertain light ahead of them. It was a cold night, and the stars seemed very high. The saloons were still. Light and sound spilled out of the Oriental across the street and the Crystal Palace on the opposite corner. The life in the saloons seemed to intensify the empty silence of the street. On the corner of Fifth Street, Huachuca Water Company had a building half built. They went in.

"Virgil would have come out of the Oriental and walked across Fifth Street," Wyatt said. "So they would have to have been standing about here. Two men with shotguns."

Morgan moved the lantern.

"No shell casings," he said. "Nobody used a Winchester."

"Goodfellow said it was all pellets," Wyatt said.

They stood looking around the partial room. It seemed colder in the empty, partly open building than it had on the street.

"Virgil's always been fine," Morgan said.

Wyatt nodded.

"Seems funny," Morgan said, "thinking about him not being fine."

"I know."

"I mean he can still shoot a Colt, I guess. But he can't shoot a rifle, can't fight a man except one-handed. I mean, it's like Virgil ain't quite there anymore."

"I know."

"I guess Virgil will still know what to do," Morgan said.

"It's not the same," Wyatt said.

"No, I guess it isn't," Morgan said.

"And it never will be."

The lantern light picked up something lying beside a stack of rough siding. Morgan went over and squatted down, holding the lantern up.

"Somebody's hat," he said and picked it up.

Wyatt squatted beside him and they examined the hat. It was like everyone's hat except that inside it, crudely burned into the leather sweatband, was a name: "I. Clanton."

"Ike," Morgan said. "Sonova bitch Ike Clanton."

"Doesn't mean he did it," Wyatt said.

"What the hell does it mean?" Morgan said. "Mean that Ike goes around, throws his hat away in empty buildings?"

"Means we got a place to start," Wyatt said.

Forty-six

Wyatt and Josie shared pigeon pie at Maison Dorée in the Cosmopolitan. Both picked at the food, without much appetite. Josie drank wine. Wyatt drank coffee.

"Virgil says he thought he might have seen Frank Stilwell scoot into the Huachuca building," Wyatt said. "Just before he got shot."

"He's with the cowboys?"

"Sure."

"You think he shot Virgil?"

"Maybe. Virgil couldn't be sure it was him."

"But you found Ike's hat," she said.

"We'll talk to Ike about that. Crawley Dake's appointed me a U.S. marshal. Means I can appoint some deputies."

"But what are you going to *do*?" Josie said.

The wine was making her impatient.

"It's what I'm trying to do," Wyatt said. "I'm trying to still be a lawman. I'm trying to find out who did what they did, and then I'm going to try and arrest them."

"And if they try to kill you again?"

"They'll try," Wyatt said.

"Kill them first," Josie said.

Wyatt put his hand over hers.

"Aren't you fierce," he said.

"I don't care anymore about anything else. Kill everyone. I don't want you hurt."

"What I need from you is to go visit your father," Wyatt said.

"I told you before, I won't leave you."

"You're not leaving me," Wyatt said. "You're leaving me free to do what I need to do without worrying about you."

"Johnny wouldn't hurt me," Josie said.

"I don't think he would," Wyatt said. "But Johnny's got something rolling downhill that he can't stop. I want you safe."

"And where do you think it will end?" Josie said.

"People got to go to jail," Wyatt said. "And some got to be shot, I expect."

"And it's harder for you if I'm here?"

"I love you," Wyatt said. "I will always love you. But, yes, it will be easier if I know you're safe."

"Then I'll go. I'll pack tonight and go tomorrow."

They were silent, most of the pigeon pie uneaten on their plates.

"How's Virgil?" Josie said finally.

"He'll be all right," Wyatt said. "He's full of morphine now. Virgil's tough. And Allie's with him."

"Allie doesn't like me," Josie said.

"No," Wyatt said. "She doesn't like me much either. But she likes Virgil."

Josie drank a little more claret.

"And how are you?" Josie said.

"Nobody shot me," Wyatt said.

"I know that Virgil was as much like a father as he was a brother."

"He's not that much older than me," Wyatt said.

"I know."

"But you're right," Wyatt said. "He's always been the one. Maybe I'm closer to Morgan, for just playing cards and talking. But it's always been Virgil. He's the one counted. We always cared what Virgil thought. Always wanted to do things the way Virgil did them. It's probably why me and Morg are gunhands, 'cause Virgil was a gunhand. Hell, now Warren's a gunhand."

"And Virgil?"

"Now he's not a gunhand anymore. I mean he can still shoot. He's got his right hand. But a man can only use one arm isn't the same in a fight. Hell, he'd have trouble reloading, according to Goodfellow."

"So he can't take care of things anymore."

"No."

"And now you are the one," Josie said.

"I guess."

Wyatt drank the rest of his coffee. Josie finished her wine.

"You want to come to my place?" Josie said. "And help me pack?"

"Yes," Wyatt said. "But you can pack later."

Josie smiled at him.

"Of course I can," she said.

Forty-seven

It was mid-March and the desert spring was already beginning to ornament the scrub around Tombstone. The window was open and the hopeful smell of it drifted into Virgil's room at the Cosmopolitan, where Wyatt and Virgil sat together. Virgil was shaved and dressed. His white shirt was freshly laundered, though he wore no collar. His face was indoor pale. The white cloth sling on his left arm was freshly laundered too. On the table near his right hand was a big single action Colt with walnut grips. They were drinking coffee.

"You miss Josie?" Virgil said.

"I do."

"Mattie's been talking to Allie. She thinks maybe she's won you back," Virgil said.

"She's got no reason to think that," Wyatt said. "I haven't been near her."

"Women think things," Virgil said.

They both drank coffee.

"Crawley Dake refused to accept that resignation letter," Wyatt said.

"I told you he would," Virgil said. "Why'd you write it, anyway?"

"Tired," Wyatt said. "Tired of listening to all that horse-shit in *The Nugget*. A little tired of guns, of my brother getting shot. A little tired of all the politics and bad-mouthing, and court appearances. Tired of Tombstone, maybe. Thinking maybe I should move along."

"I'm a little tired of your brother getting shot too," Virgil said.

"Well, I'm not going nowhere until we clean that up, deputy marshal or not."

"Making any progress?"

"Not a lot to show for three months' posse work," Wyatt said.

"You got Ike in jail."

"I do. But he won't cooperate. He denies having anything to do with shooting you, and he goddamned insists that he don't know who did. I even tried telling him we could make a deal."

"Bygones be bygones?"

"Something like that."

"He say anything about giving me back my left arm?" Virgil said.

Wyatt smiled slightly.

"Didn't say I meant it 'bout bygones."

Virgil smiled too.

"But he didn't bite."

"No," Wyatt said. "Fact is, he's swearing out a warrant on us for killing Billy and the McLaurys."

"He's wasting his time," Virgil said.

"And ours."

"Which may be the point. You keep showing up in court, you ain't out chasing down the cowboys."

"Tom Fitch'll do most of the appearing in court for us." Virgil drank some coffee.

"Still, Ike's an irritating little bastard," Virgil said.

"Probably Behan's idea on the warrant," Wyatt said. "Keeps the cowboys stirred up. Ringo's in town, and Curley Bill and Frank Stilwell."

"I thought you had John Ringo for holding up the stage."

"Driver wouldn't identify him."

"Scared of Ringo?"

"Yep."

"Can't blame him that much, I guess."

Virgil leaned back a little in his chair. Wyatt noticed that he seemed to move without pain.

"Allie," Virgil shouted. "We need some more coffee."

Virgil's wife came in from the parlor with a big enamel coffeepot and poured some for both of them. She bent over and kissed Virgil on the top of the head and went out.

"Seems to like you better than she likes me," Wyatt said.

"That's a fact," Virgil said.

"Fact she don't like me much at all."

"No," Virgil said, "she don't."

"Ever since Josie."

"Yep. Feels bad for Mattie."

"Hell, Virg, she don't even like Mattie."

"She likes her better now that she's a woman scorned."

"She blame me for you getting shot?" Wyatt said.

"Yes."

"I guess she's got the right. It goes back to me taking Josie from Behan."

"Everything goes back to something," Virgil said. "What matters here, whatever Allie feels, is that our names are Earp. You and me and Morgan and Warren and James. We are brothers. We are made of the same stuff. That's what we go back to."

"I know."

"You want Josie. I want Josie. Morg wants Josie. James and Warren want Josie. People don't like it, they don't like us. You do something. We do it with you. Brothers. The Earp brothers."

"I know."

"Don't never think anything else is true," Virgil said. "That's who we are. That's what we got. It's what we always had. Before the women came. Before any of us ever shot a gun. If I got shot on account of something you did, it's because that's what I'm supposed to do. Don't matter if Allie likes it. She loves me. I love her. But that don't matter either. Blood, Wyatt. Flesh and blood."

Wyatt stared at his brother. In his life it was probably the longest uninterrupted set of sentences Virgil had ever spoken. He spoke softly, without heat, almost as if he were thinking aloud. Allie came in as he finished.

"You need anything else, Virgil?" she said.

"No," Virgil said.

He put his right arm around her waist.

"I got everything I need," Virgil said.

Forty-eight

As they came out of the theater, Wyatt took the Colt .45 he had under his coat and put it in the side pocket of his slicker.

Morgan saw the transfer.

"You thinking there might be trouble, Wyatt?" Morgan said.

"There's talk," Wyatt said. "Goodrich thinks there might be trouble."

"Well, hell, Wyatt," Morgan said. "It's Saturday night. There's supposed to be trouble."

"Just don't button your gun up so tight you can't get it out quick," Wyatt said.

Morgan laughed, and they stepped into the street. With his left hand, Wyatt yanked his hat down hard over his forehead. Driven by a wind from the south, the cold spring rain came hard and straight at them as he and Morgan walked up Fourth Street toward Allen. Sherman McMasters and Dan Tipton walked a step behind them.

"*Stolen Kisses,*" Morgan said happily. "Goddamn!"

"Pretty good show," Wyatt said.

"Maybe I'll see it again tomorrow," Morgan said. "How long's it running."

"Through the twentieth of March," McMasters said.

He spoke loudly, forcing his voice through the wind and rain.

"What's today?" Morgan said.

"Eighteenth," Wyatt said. "You got till Monday."

They turned left at Allen. The rain was just as hard, but the wind was diverted some by the buildings now as they walked east on Allen.

"How about a little whiskey," Morgan said. "And some pool."

"How about a lot of whiskey and some pool," McMasters said.

"Sounds even better," Morgan said, and they turned in at Campbell and Hatch's Saloon. In the back where the pool tables were, McMasters and Tipton concentrated on whiskey. Wyatt drank coffee and watched while Morgan, his drink sitting on the edge of the table, played his second game with Robert Hatch, who owned the place. Some of the other drinkers had gathered to watch. The back door had a four-pane glass window. The bottom two were painted over, the top two clear. The wind rattled the door and the rain spattered hard against the glass, showing in thick, short streams as it ran down the clear glass. But the window was tight. The stove was working full out. George Berry, standing near it, had steam coming off of his wet mackinaw. The room was warm.

Hatch left the six ball teetering at the edge of the far corner pocket. Morgan smiled.

"Tough shot, Bob," Morgan said. "What a shame."

He leaned over the table behind the cue ball, sighting the shot.

"Six in the corner," he said.

One of the windowpanes exploded and Morgan sprawled across the table. Near the stove Berry staggered as the same bullet took him in the thigh. Morgan gasped. Wyatt had his Colt half out when a second shot drove into the wall above his head. Wyatt lunged to the pool table beside Morgan and threw himself partly over him. The Colt was all the way out now, and he stared into the wet wind that surged in through the shattered glass. McMasters yanked the door open, and he and Hatch rushed out into the rain.

"Get Goodfellow," Wyatt yelled. "Goddammit, get Goodfellow."

By the time Goodfellow got there, Morgan had been moved to the couch in Hatch's card room. Goodfellow knelt beside him and looked. He put a hand on Morgan's shoulder and stood up. Goodfellow didn't say anything. Wyatt didn't ask anything. They both knew what there was to know. Another doctor arrived to examine George Berry's leg. Slowed by its passage through Morgan, the bullet had barely lodged in Berry's thigh. The doctor took it out with an extractor and bandaged the wound. Wyatt crouched beside his brother; Morgan was breathing badly. He didn't try to talk. He knew what Wyatt knew. They had both seen too many men shot dead to be fooled this time. Virgil and Allie came in. James and Bessie arrived. Wyatt stayed with his head next to Morgan's. Once Morgan whispered to him. Wyatt nodded and whispered back and then everyone was quiet.

"Are my legs out straight?" Morgan said softly.

"Yes."

No one said anything else. Allie and Bessie cried softly. And Morgan died.

CHRONICLE

FOR VIOLATING THE NEUTRALITY LAWS
Philadelphia, October 26—
Captain A. C. Rand and Mate, Thomas Pender, of the steamer Tropic, who were convicted in the United States District Court of violating the neutrality laws by furnishing arms and ammunition to insurgents in Haiti, were today sentenced by Judge Butler to one year's imprisonment each and to pay a fine of $500 and the cost of the prosecution.

* * *

HALLER ONE OF QUANTRELL'S BORDER HEROES
Denver, Oct. 26—
The killing of his wife, Alice Haller, by Johnston Haller, and the wounding of the man Morris, who had won the affections of Alice, has brought to light a story which began in a border romance and has ended in disgrace to two and sorrow to a third. Haller was a member of the Quantrell crowd, and a knight of the road when Jesse and Frank James were looked upon with a sort of mock heroism. He was a fearless devil, and in the saddle he was handsome as Murat. He was in some of the bloodiest engagements that

blighted the West. He went with Quantrell, when that daring horseman swooped down upon Lawrence, Kan. and left the bloodstains of its best people on the blackened ruins of their homes. He was also a trusted courier of the James boys. . . .

* * *

A LEGACY FOR A COLORED WOMAN
New York, October 26—
The following letter was received at police headquarters today, dated Powhatan, VA, October 23, 1883: "A colored woman named Flora Baker left Richmond some years ago to seek employment as a domestic servant. She had a couple of children whom she took with her. She is probably in New York City, or in Brooklyn. A legacy has been left by her old master, W. W. Wooldridge, and if you can find her, I will compensate you handsomely." It is signed W. Pope Dubary.

* * *

CARRIED AWAY BY ANGELS
Baltimore, October 26—
Mrs. David Moses, the fat bride weighing 517 pounds, on exhibition here, and recently married in New York, was found dead in bed this morning. She had been in

it for two weeks, and not been on exhibition since last Tuesday. She was born in Detroit in 1866 and had been before the public for about a year. She had gained sixty-seven pounds in the past seven months. She was to have appeared in Philadelphia next Monday at a museum whose curiosity hall is in the fourth story of the building. As she could not walk up three flights, the manager was putting up a derrick for purposes of hoisting her.

* * *

BASE BALL GROUNDS,
Friday Oct. 27th
Bostons vs. Dr. Pope's Picked Nine.

* * *

GLOBE THEATER—EXTRA
Mr. Jon Stetson has the honor to announce the engagement of Mr. Edwin Booth under the management of Messrs. Brooks & Dickson, commencing Monday, Nov. 5 in the following repertoire.

*Monday and Tuesday, Nov. 5 and 6—*RICHELIEU. *Wednesday, Nov. 7—*MACBETH. *Thursday and Friday, Nov. 8 and 9—*KING LEAR. *Saturday Matinee, Nov. 10—*RICHELIEU.

* * *

The young man void of understanding may be depended upon to fall into the ditch of debauchery without much pushing, and the gilded youth will seek out white sepulchers without other urging than their own fondness for folly, but the stranger must be enticed into the snares of the strange woman by cunning wiles. Not long ago Lillie DeLacy found it advisable to move out of a street at the South End, where the neighbors objected to her nocturnal festivities, and open a new establishment on Eliot St. In order to get the place upon a paying basis she sent cards through the mails to such persons who seemed most likely to accept invitations to call upon a strange woman, but these cards did not all fall into the hands of strangers from the country. The police got hold of some of them and detectives called at the house to investigate. The result was Lillie's arraignment in court for keeping a house of ill-fame, but as the only evidence was her own admission to the detectives, which was not legally sufficient, she was discharged. It is very wrong in Lillie to carry on such a business, without doubt, but there are grounds for suspecting that several other persons in this city are engaged in similar pursuits and are never interfered with by virtuous administrators of the law.

Forty-nine

A *half hour* after Morgan Earp died, Doc Holliday, in a black hat and no slicker, with half a quart of whiskey in him, and the bottle in his left hand, started to look for Johnny Behan.

"It was him killed Morgan, him and Will McLaury," Doc said. "I don't know they pulled the trigger, but they done it, either way."

With the rain coming hard and the wind pushing at him, he walked up Allen Street armed with a Colt .45 on his hip and a Smith & Wesson hammerless .32 in a shoulder rig. Every door he came to he opened. If a door was locked he would kick it in, and curse the people whom he often rousted out of bed. In the saloons even the nastiest or drunkest of the patrons had nothing to say to him. His eyes were bottomless, his face was ashen. His clothing was soaked and his face was wet. Occasionally he stopped to pull at the whiskey bottle. When it was empty he threw it against the side of a saloon and watched it shatter. Then he went into the gaslight and reeking stove heat and took a nearly full bottle off the bar and drank some and scanned the room.

"Johnny Behan," he shouted. "Behan, you back-shooting son of a bitch."

Behan was not in the room. No one said anything. Doc rushed out, his Colt hanging loosely in his right hand, his left with a new bottle of whiskey. He didn't pay for the whiskey. No one asked him to. He continued up Allen past Sixth Street and started kicking in doors in the cribs where the whores were. Behan wasn't there. Neither was Will McLaury. Doc turned toward Toughnut Street where the miners lived. Again he banged on doors and pushed in past whoever answered. All night he rambled through Tombstone in the harsh rain with his gun in his hand, drinking, looking for Behan. Near dawn he stood in the middle of Fremont Street in front of the San Jose Rooming House and turned his face up to the downpour and screamed, "Behan," at the black sky. Then he stumbled back down Fremont to Fourth Street and up Fourth into the face of the storm toward the Cosmopolitan Hotel. In the lobby he tossed the partly drunk whiskey bottle onto the lobby floor. The remaining whiskey spilled silently onto the carpet as Doc climbed the stairs to his room and went in and fell facedown on his bed, where he lay motionless, the Colt in his hand, his clothes soaked with rainwater, and cried.

Fifty

It was morning. The early sun shone straight down Allen Street. In Hafford's, Virgil and Wyatt were drinking coffee. Wyatt had some paper and a short pencil.

"It's Stilwell," Virgil said. "Everybody in town knows it was him. It was pretty surely him I saw heading toward the waterworks the night they shot me."

Wyatt wrote down Stilwell's name.

"Which means it was Behan," Wyatt said.

"Stilwell's his deputy."

Wyatt wrote *Behan* on the paper.

"And Pete Spence and Indian Charlie."

"That's the talk."

Wyatt wrote those names.

"McLaury was gone for two days when they shot Morgan," Wyatt said. "He's out of it."

"Ike?" Virgil said.

"Nobody thinks so," Virgil said.

Wyatt wrote down his name.

"Put him down anyway, in case I come across him."

"Nobody be mad at you for shooting Ike," Virgil said. "Sooner or later you're going to have to deal with Curley Bill and Ringo."

"I know."

"People been coming to see me all night," Virgil said. "There's talk they were in on it."

"Nothing much happens with the cowboys that Bill and Ringo don't want to happen. Behan don't do much that they don't want done."

"I know."

"And they're tight with Stilwell. You bring him down, they're going to be looking for you."

"They'll be able to find me," Wyatt said.

"Stay away from Behan," Virgil said. "What with you romancing his woman, it'll look like you murdered him to get her."

Wyatt didn't say anything. His face was expressionless.

"Besides which, he's still the sheriff," Virgil said. "Even Crawley can't smooth it over if you shoot the sheriff."

Wyatt nodded.

"I won't drag her into this," Wyatt said. "I kill anybody, it won't be over Josie."

Virgil nodded as if to himself. He rubbed his good hand over his jaw as though to see if he needed a shave.

"You know, and I know, that this is about Josie," Virgil said. "You may have to kill Behan. If you're too certain you won't, he may get to kill you."

"I won't have to kill him," Wyatt said. "Behan's got no spine for coming at me alone."

"He ain't alone," Virgil said.

"He will be," Wyatt said.

Virgil stared for a time at his brother.

"You're going to kill them all," Virgil said.

"All I can find," Wyatt said.

"Legal?" Virgil said.

"No. I am not a lawman now. I'm Morgan Earp's brother."

"And mine," Virgil said softly.

Fifty-one

Morgan's body went to Benson in the horse-drawn hearse at the head of a funeral procession. The casket was loaded into a boxcar at Benson and taken to Tucson, where it was transferred onto the train to California. James and Bessie, Virgil and Allie would take it from there to their parents' home in Colton.

The Earp men were armed. Virgil and James with handguns. Wyatt and Warren with handguns and shotguns. Doc Holliday was with them, and Sherman McMasters and Turkey Creek Jack Johnson. A telegraph clerk at Tucson wired reports of men, searching all incoming trains, striding through the cars with sawed-off shotguns under their coats. Armed men gathered and dispersed near the Tucson Railroad Station. Everyone talked of the Earps coming in with Morgan's body. Frank Stilwell was there, to meet a deputy sheriff, he said.

At 6:45 in the evening everybody that was going aboard was on the California train except the Earp party. Doc Holliday and Turkey Creek Jack Johnson boarded the train, walked in opposite directions through the car where the Earps would sit, and posted themselves in the adjacent cars by the doors on either side of the Earp's car. Doc carried a 10-gauge. Turkey Creek Jack Johnson had a Winchester. Sherman McMasters got on with them and walked through the entire train with a shotgun. At the back he leaned out and yelled "Clear" to Wyatt, who stood with his family.

James and Bessie, Virgil and Allie climbed up onto the train from whose stack the smoke was already pouring. Wyatt and Warren stood on either side of the train steps with shotguns, then followed them. When the departing Earps were seated, Doc and Turkey Creek Jack stepped down onto the platform on either side of the train and watched in both directions to see that no one else got on.

"Once the doors close and you're underway, you're out of it," Wyatt said.

"Sure thing," Virgil said. "Besides, I can still shoot."

"But you can't reload in anything under an hour," Warren said.

"Means I can get the first six," Virgil said. "If there's more, James will have to clean up."

James smiled. But it was a thin smile. He was brave enough, Wyatt thought, but whatever happened in the war had taken it out of him. He wasn't a shooter. Still, he'd do what he had to. Wyatt was sure of that.

"Hell, I'd turn Allie on them," Wyatt said.

Allie smiled at him.

"We ain't always got along, Wyatt. And I've been ready to tell you when I didn't like what you done."

"That's true," Wyatt said.

"But you take care of yourself doing what it is you're going to do."

"I will, Allie."

Her eyes were teary.

"I don't want to lose you too," Allie said and stood and put her arms around Wyatt. He patted her back.

"You too, Warren. You be very damned careful."

"It's the cowboys," Warren said, "that need to be careful."

The conductor stopped in front of Wyatt.

"Trains all locked down," he said. "'Cept this car. Time to go."

Wyatt nodded and looked at his brothers.

"See you in a little while," Wyatt said.

He looked at Virgil. Virgil nodded. He put the Colt in his lap and put out his working hand. Wyatt took it. Then he and Warren left the train and watched as the conductor bolted the door. The engine whistled and the boiler huffed faster. McMasters jumped off the rear of the last car. Turkey Creek Jack Johnson walked back toward him. Warren followed. Doc began to walk along the train toward Wyatt. Across the next set of tracks, near an empty train at rest on its siding, there was a flurry of movement. Two men disappeared behind the train, but the third man stood there and Wyatt saw him.

"Stilwell," Wyatt said and began to move toward him. Stilwell ran. Wyatt followed. Suddenly, as he came up against the engine of the silent train, Stilwell stopped and turned. Wyatt was fifteen feet away. He kept coming. Stilwell seemed frozen. At three feet, Wyatt stopped. The shotgun was level with Stilwell's chest. Both hammers were back.

Stilwell said, "Morg."

And again, "Morg," and grabbed at the shotgun. Wyatt pulled the trigger, and the right barrel pounded a near-solid cluster of shotgun pellets into Stilwell's chest. He was probably dead before the second barrel went off. Doc Holliday came up behind Wyatt at a dead run. Wyatt was already reloading the shotgun. Doc looked down at Stilwell's body and drew his Colt and fired five shots into it. Then he, too, began to reload.

Behind them, the wheels of the train to California began to turn. The train strained into motion. Wyatt ran alongside it, and as Virgil peered out the now moving window Wyatt held up his right hand with one finger raised. Inside the train Virgil nodded. He understood. Wyatt had gotten one of them. For Morg.

Fifty-two

They were back in the Cosmopolitan Hotel the next day. All men now. The women were gone. Wyatt and Doc and Warren. Texas Jack and Turkey Creek Jack and Sherman McMasters. They always had revolvers with them. They always carried long guns. Doc was at a table in the bar drinking whiskey when Wyatt came in. Wyatt leaned his Winchester against the table and sat down.

"Amazing," Doc said, "how a few gunshots clear everything up."

The barman brought Wyatt coffee.

"Now it's all out in the open and aboveboard and right in front," Doc said. "You against Behan. Earps against cowboys. Republicans against Democrats. *The Epitaph* against *The Nugget*. Now everybody wants to look can see what they want to see."

Wyatt drank his coffee.

"You know Behan put Stilwell up to shooting Morgan, and you know it was because Morgan knocked him on his ass when he come bothering Josie. You know he's in on them stage robberies, Wyatt. You know he's getting a nice slice of the cattle rustling out of Mexico. You know him and Ringo and Curley Bill are tighter than the valve on a virgin."

"Got a copy of the coroner's report on Morgan," Wyatt said.

He was holding the thick, white coffee mug in both hands and staring over the top of it through the saloon doors out at the little stretch of Allen Street that showed under them.

"Says Stilwell, Spence, Hank Swilling, Indian Charlie, and somebody named Fries are the main suspects for shooting Morgan. Gives Indian Charlie's real name in there, Florentine Cruz. Never knew Charlie's name was Florentine Cruz."

"We knew the rest pretty much anyway, didn't we?" Doc said.

He picked up the whiskey bottle and splashed a little more into his glass.

"I'm putting together a posse," Wyatt said. "Heard that Spence and Indian Charlie are out at Spence's wood camp."

The steam from the coffee whispered up past his face.

"I'll be in the street on horseback at nine this morning. I'd be pleased if you'd join me."

"You promise me I can shoot one of 'em?" Doc said.

" 'Less they shoot you first," Wyatt said.

Doc drank off the newly poured whiskey. He smiled.

"No, Wyatt, I'll shoot one of them unless they *kill* me first."

"Nine o'clock," Wyatt said. "Be ready to stay out awhile."

At nine in the morning Wyatt was there on Allen Street up on the blue roan gelding with the sun at his back. He had a Colt .45 and a .45 Winchester rifle, and a lot of ammunition in the saddlebags. He had a blanket roll tied behind his saddle, and a pack mule on a lead. Warren was up beside him, smaller than Wyatt and dark. Doc was there mounted, as were McMasters and Turkey Creek Jack Johnson, looking too big for the small bay mare he rode. Texas Jack Vermilion had a rifle and a shotgun in saddle scabbards. Vermilion sported a flamboyant mustache.

Wyatt handed the pack mule lead line to McMasters.

"You can ride drag for a while, Sherm," he said.

As McMasters led the mule to the back of the group, John Behan came up Allen Street. Billy Breakenridge was with him, and Dave Neagle. Wyatt nodded to Neagle.

"Morning, Dave," Wyatt said.

Neagle nodded back at Wyatt.

"Dave don't look so comfortable," Warren murmured. "He scared?"

"Dave's never scared," Wyatt said. "Probably embarrassed at being with Johnny."

"You fellas going someplace?" Behan said.

He was smiling. No one answered him.

"Anyplace special?" Behan said.

Breakenridge and Neagle stood on either side of him a few feet from him. Both wore deputy badges. Both wore Colts. Neagle's eyes moved steadily as he looked at all five of the horsemen.

"Wyatt, I need to see you," Behan said.

No one spoke. Wyatt looked at Behan. His gaze was heavy. It was as if Behan could feel the weight of it. He didn't move, but he looked like he wished to back up. The silence lengthened awkwardly. Finally Wyatt broke it.

"About what?" Wyatt said.

"About killing Frank Stilwell," Behan said.

"You are going to see me once too many times, Johnny," he said.

Behind Wyatt his party began to spread out. Doc sidled his horse left, Warren right. The pack mule wouldn't move sideways, so Vermilion stayed with it where he was. But Mc-Masters and Turkey Creek Jack moved wider still so that the Earp party was now in a wedge-shaped phalanx.

"I will talk with Paul," Wyatt said. "Next time I'm in Tucson."

Behan didn't say anything. Wyatt made a small clicking noise and tapped the roan with his knee. The roan moved forward and the rest of the horses moved after them. The pack mule had no objection to moving forward and joined the rest of the party as the horses walked on past Behan and his deputies. Wyatt lit a cigar carefully, turning it to get it right, then when it was going as he wanted it. He clicked to the roan again and the horses broke into a trot as they turned onto Third Street and out of sight, as Behan, watching them go, could see them no more.

"Who's Paul?" Warren said.

"Bob Paul. Sheriff in Pima County."

"Why'll you talk to him?"

"Well," Wyatt said, "it's his jurisdiction . . ."

Wyatt drew on his cigar and let the smoke out slowly. The horses were eager in the early desert spring, tossing their heads and arching their necks to strain against the reins as the posse moved out of town.

"And," Wyatt said, "he's a real lawman."

"Unlike Mr. Behan," Doc said.

"He ain't a real anything," Warren said.

At the back, holding the pack mule, McMasters raised his voice.

"Why don't we just plug him, Wyatt."

"We won't plug him," Wyatt said.

Fifty-three

They camped that night a few miles north of Tombstone, sleeping close to the fire in the still, cold night.

"Got the coroner's report," Wyatt said to no one in particular. "Says that most likely the people who killed Morgan are Frank Stilwell . . ."

"The late Frank Stilwell," Doc said softly.

". . . Peter Spence, Fries, Swilling and Florentine Cruz."

"Cruz?" McMasters said.

"Indian Charlie," Johnson said.

"That's all," Doc said.

"That's all they named as suspects," Wyatt said.

"You know Curley Bill was in it, and Ringo," Doc said. "And you know that goddamned weasel Behan was behind it."

"Don't know that for sure," Wyatt said. "But we'll ride over to Spence's lumber camp tomorrow. See if somebody there will tell us."

"Should we take turns on guard?" Vermilion said.

"No need," Wyatt said. "Doc sleeps so light he can hear a rattlesnake yawn."

"Can't tell I'm asleep," Doc said, "'less I dream."

He took a pull on a whiskey bottle he had taken from his saddlebag.

"That help you to stay awake, Doc?" Turkey Creek said.

"That helps me stay alive," Doc said and handed the bottle to Johnson, who took a pull and passed it to Vermilion.

The bottle went around the campfire for a while, skipping Wyatt each time, until one by one, wrapped in their blankets under the infinite sky, close to the fire, they went to sleep and Doc alone sat awake, alone with the bottle.

In the morning they ate bacon and biscuits, drank coffee—Doc added whiskey to his—and rode east toward the Dragoon Mountains, with their hats tilted forward to keep the sun out of their eyes. The horses picked their way carefully through the low, harsh brush. A hawk cruised soundlessly in the high sky. Doc sipped whiskey from a bottle in his saddlebags. Wyatt knew that Doc hated quiet. He'd start talking soon. Doc talking was something to hear. He talked about guns and dental tools and Catholic theology, and whores, and people he'd shot, and meals he had eaten, and cards he had held, and the nature of man, and why it was best to steam Prairie Chicken before you roasted it.

As they started up the long gradual rise toward Spence's wood-cutting operation, Doc said, "Where's your ladies, Wyatt?"

"Josie's in San Francisco," Wyatt said. "With her father."

"How 'bout Mattie?"

"Gone to my mother's place in California."

"Funny thing," Doc said, "you hadn't taken up with Josie Marcus, we wouldn't be out here riding down the people killed Morgan."

The horses were blowing as they shuffled up the long grade. There was only the sound of the horses' hooves, the jangle of harness metal, the creak of saddle leather.

"Talk about something else, Doc," Wyatt said.

Fifty-four

They reached the top of the long rise and looked down into the valley where Spence's wood-cutting operation was set up next to a stand of timber.

"We'll circle," Wyatt said, "so we don't come at them with the sun in our eyes."

The horses strung out single file as they moved down the valley side and away from the wood choppers. When they were on the other side Wyatt turned them toward the camp, straight west, so that the sun would be at his back and straight into the eyes of the people in the wood camp. McMasters took his Winchester from the saddle boot and rested it across the pommel. Doc had a shotgun across his saddle.

There was a Mexican cutting and stacking wood.

"You speak English?" Wyatt said.

The Mexican shook his head. He was frightened. Wyatt turned to McMasters.

"Ask him where Cruz is, and Spence."

McMasters spoke to the Mexican man. He answered, pointing toward the northern slope of the valley.

"Says Spence is in Tombstone with Behan. Says Indian Charlie's over that hill rounding up some strays."

Wyatt turned the aging roan horse and rode toward the hill without a word. The rest of the men followed, catching up to him, and spreading out on either side of him. They went up the hillside and over it. There were other hills beyond it. A teamster named Judah was driving stock across their path. With him was a Mexican named Acosta.

"You know where Pete Spence is?" Wyatt said.

His voice was flat and easy, as if he didn't really care where Spence was.

"I thought he was in Tombstone."

"You a friend of his?" Wyatt said.

Judah showed no sign that he thought the question a dangerous one to answer.

"Known Spence a long time," Judah said.

"You seen Indian Charlie around?"

"Cruz? Over there someplace," Judah said. "Looking for a couple mules that went roaming."

Wyatt nodded, clucked softly to the roan and rode toward the next hill. The other riders stayed with him, spread out on either side. Judah and Acosta both watched them as they went.

"Trouble," Judah said.

Acosta nodded.

As Wyatt and the other riders topped the next hill, Indian Charlie was on the downslope hazing two mules ahead of him. When he saw Wyatt he turned and ran.

"Knock him down, Sherm," Wyatt said. "Don't kill him."

McMasters reined the horse still, levered a round up in the Winchester, aimed carefully and shot Cruz in the right leg. The sound made the two mules scatter, one of them kicking his back heels. The impact of the bullet sent Cruz sprawling face forward, and when they came up to him he was lying on his back with the blood slowly staining his trouser leg.

"Talk to him, Sherm. Tell him we know he killed Morgan. Ask him who else done it."

McMasters slid the Winchester back into the saddle scabbard and spoke to Cruz. Cruz answered at length, moving his hands, his dark eyes wide and eager, and full of fear. The rest of the posse sat silently, letting their horses crop the grass. They weren't up very high, but the air in the mountains seemed cooler to Wyatt, fresher, as if it had more movement behind it than the air around Tombstone, like the difference between standing water and running water. Wyatt sat motionless in the saddle, while Cruz talked to McMasters.

"He never killed anybody," McMasters said. "That's what he says. Says he just went along to make sure they got the right man. Spence didn't know you. This guy says he knew both you and Morgan. Says him, Spence and Stilwell, and somebody named Swilling, met Curley Bill, and Ringo, back of the courthouse; they heard that you'd gone to bed, and Morg was at Hatch's. So they decided to kill Morg and they went up there. Then some guy named Fries comes up and says that you hadn't gone to bed, that you were in Hatch's too. But Curley Bill, and Stilwell, and Swilling went into the alley back of Hatch's, and he says he heard shooting and everybody come running out."

McMasters paused, as if he had forgotten. He spoke to Cruz in Spanish. Cruz replied.

"They all went to Frank Patterson's ranch to fix up an alibi, and Stilwell says he shot Morgan, Curley Bill and Swilling say they shot too, but missed, and Stilwell says that made two Earps he'd shot."

"Virgil," Wyatt said with no inflection.

Cruz spoke again. When he was through, McMasters didn't speak.

"What'd he say?" Wyatt asked.

"Says he got nothing against you or your brothers. He didn't want to do you no harm."

"So why did he?" Wyatt said.

Again McMasters didn't say anything.

"Ask him that," Wyatt said.

His voice was as hard and flat and brittle as a piece of slate.

McMasters shrugged, and spoke again to Cruz. Cruz answered. When he translated, McMasters's face was blank and his voice was without inflection.

"Says they give him a twenty-five-dollar watch."

"Twenty-five dollars," Wyatt said.

McMasters nodded. The other riders didn't speak or move. They could hear the wind moving softly among the trees into the timber stand. Doc's horse, snuffling in the grass, inhaled something and snorted it out. Otherwise, the silence seemed impenetrable.

"For Morgan Earp," Wyatt said.

"Wyatt," Doc said.

The gun was in Wyatt's hand almost as if it had always been there. Cruz saw the movement and put his arm up as if it could protect him. Wyatt shot Cruz in the head, and as Cruz fell backward, he shot him twice more. Cruz lay on his back, his arm thrown across his face. The horses had heard gunfire before. They stood stolidly as the explosions echoed across the empty mountain valley, rolling past Judah and Acosta a half mile away, looking down from the next hilltop.

Fifty-five

"Dick Wright says Behan's got a posse out for us. Says there's a warrant out of Tombstone for you killing Stilwell."

"Dick bring the money?" Wyatt said.

"Yes," Warren said. "Right when he said he would."

"Crawley Dake's money?" Doc asked.

"Didn't say," Warren answered.

"It'd be Crawley's," Wyatt said. "Federal funds."

"Well, you're in it now," Doc said as they made camp near the water hole at Iron Springs, twelve miles north of Tombstone. The night was clear and the stars were high and uninterested in the velvety blackness. The silence was vast, though, Wyatt thought, in fact, when people talk about silence they really mean human sound. They don't notice the sounds that were there before they came. That will be there after they're gone. Night birds. Coyotes. The scurry of small animals in the brush. A breeze stirring the scrub growth. The crackle of the fire seemed to drown all that out unless you listened. Texas Jack was cooking salt pork in a heavy black-iron fry pan. Doc had the bottle out, and it moved from man to man, skipping Wyatt.

"Go easy on that stuff, Warren," Wyatt said as his brother took the bottle. Warren drank some whiskey and passed the bottle to Turkey Creek Jack.

"Not easy," Warren said, "your brother being a parson."

"Not easy being your brother," Wyatt said and smiled.

Doc was drunk. He was probably always a little drunk. But when he was more than a little drunk, Wyatt knew it because his stubbornness increased.

"You done it to yourself, Wyatt," Doc said. "You come over to my side, you can't go back."

He took out the Colt .45 he had used to shoot Florentine Cruz, and flipped the cylinder open.

"I'm going where I got to go, Doc. Things don't give me much choice."

Wyatt took the big flat-nosed .45 bullets from the cylinder and put them one at a time into the ammunition loops on his belt.

"It was one thing in Tombstone," Doc said. "You were a lawman. And Frank Stilwell was threatening your brothers in Tucson. But Indian Charlie . . . back there . . . that didn't have anything to do with the law."

Wyatt ran an oily cloth patch down the barrel of the Colt.

"The law had its chance," Wyatt said.

Doc took a pull of whiskey and swallowed and put his head back and laughed.

"Now it's your law," Doc said.

Wyatt didn't say anything. Texas Jack spread the fried salt pork over an inverted pot to drain, and dropped sourdough in small spoonfuls into the hot salt-pork fat.

"And," Doc took another drink, "here's the thing, parson. It's the same goddamned law as my law."

Wyatt carefully ran the patch through each of the six chambers in the cylinder. Then he carefully balled up the oily patch and put it in the fire.

"No, Doc. It's not. We got different reasons for what we do."

Wyatt put a dry patch on the short cleaning rod and ran it down the gun barrel.

"You'll shoot a man for spilling his drink," Wyatt said.

"Maybe so," Doc said. "Maybe so."

Doc passed the whiskey bottle to McMasters and leaned back against his saddle. Wyatt discarded the second patch into the fire, put his thumbnail on the muzzle and examined the barrel in the reflected firelight.

"But you won't be able to come back from this," Doc said. "Maybe we're as different as you say. But you're on my side of the line now, and there's no way to get back."

Wyatt was satisfied with the condition of the Colt. He took the bullets from his cartridge belt again, one at a time, and stood them on a rock near him, nose up. Texas Jack put some fried pork and biscuits on a tin plate and handed it to Doc.

He said, "Eat something, Doc. It'll make you stop talking for a while."

Doc took the plate and ate with his fingers. Texas Jack dished out for the others. Everyone except Wyatt ate in silence for a time. Wyatt put his plate aside until he finished with the Colt. He was running another clean patch through the barrel. Doc finished chewing. He took a drink of whiskey.

"I'm right, though," he said, "and Wyatt knows it."

Wyatt picked up the fat .45 bullets one at a time from the rock where they stood and fed them, one at a time, into the cylinder. Then he snapped the cylinder shut, put the gun back in his belt, and picked up his plate.

"I like fried biscuits," he said.

Fifty-six

For breakfast they had coffee and the last night's left-over biscuits, and Wyatt sent Warren back to wait for Dick Wright again.

"How come I got to go?" Warren said. "Wright already brought the money."

"We need to know what's happening in town," Wyatt said. "Need to know if the cowboys are there or somewhere else."

"I don't want to miss no action," Warren said.

"You're twenty-five," Wyatt said. "You got plenty of time for action."

Warren was a little sullen as he rode away, but Wyatt knew he'd do what he was told.

"Outta harm's way?" Doc said as they rode down toward the watering hole.

"I lost all the brothers I'm ready to lose," Wyatt said.

The horses smelled the water and quickened their pace. The roan got there first. As the roan started to drink, Wyatt swung down from the saddle to wash up. He loosened his gun belt. From across the spring, there was gunfire.

The other riders spun their horses and headed for cover in the cottonwoods that grew around the spring. Wyatt held the reins in his left hand. The loosened gun belt slid down over his thighs and hampered his movements as Wyatt tried to pull his Winchester from the saddle scabbard.

For Christ sake. Am I going to get shot because my gun belt fell down?

He managed to fumble the shotgun off the near side of his saddle as the roan tossed his head and twisted against the reins. Wyatt couldn't get the Winchester out. Instead he fumbled the 10-gauge Wells Fargo shotgun from the near side of the saddle and cocked it and tried to aim over the tossing back of his horse. Across the water hole, clear as day, and slowed down like everything always did in a shooting, he could see Curley Bill aiming at him with another shotgun. There were other cowboys firing. Bullets tugged at his clothing. But Wyatt saw Curley Bill as if through crystal. He could see the Wells Fargo medallion in the stock of the shotgun. Just like the one he held.

Like mine. Bill took it off a stage.

Wyatt gently eased the front sight down on the middle of Curley Bill's mass. Bill fired and the shot sang around him. A shotgun wasn't so good at this range. But it was what they had. As Curley Bill broke the shotgun to reload,

Wyatt squeezed off one barrel, then the other. Curley Bill seemed to shrink in on himself. Wyatt could see the blood suddenly brighten Bill's shirt, then he sank from sight into the low growth under the trees along the water. Behind him Wyatt heard the loud sharp sound that Winchesters make coming from the cover of the cottonwoods behind him. He could hear Doc's voice mixed in with the rifle fire.

"Wyatt, get the fuck out of there."

Covered by the rifle fire, Wyatt dropped the shotgun, hitched up his gun belt, got hold of the roan's mane, and heaved himself up onto the frantic horse. Something hammered the heel of his right boot. His leg went numb. He yanked the roan's head around and rammed him into the trees on a dead run. In the shelter of the trees he dismounted, hitched the still-panicky roan to a tree, and, crouching, moved back toward the water with a Colt in his hand. His posse was on the ground, spread out, each with a Winchester. The levered shells scattered brightly on the leaf mold around them. The gunfire stopped. There was uncertain movement across the water, then the sound of horses, and then silence and the reek of spent ammunition. The silence seemed to spiral around them. Wyatt could hear Doc's breathing.

"They've scooted," Texas Jack said.

His voice was hoarse. So was Sherman McMasters's.

"You see who it was?" McMasters said.

"Curley Bill was one of them," Wyatt said.

"You hit anyone?" Doc said.

"Curley Bill, straight on in the chest," Wyatt said. "Both barrels."

"Curley Bill's dead?"

"Be surprised if he wasn't," Wyatt said.

"Shit!" Turkey Creek Jack Johnson said. "I always kind of liked Bill."

"Fuck him," Doc said. "Let's take a look."

"You and I'll look, Doc," Wyatt said. "The rest of you boys stay ready in case they didn't all scoot."

Doc and Wyatt walked around the water hole. The cowboys were gone, including Curley Bill. At the spot where Wyatt estimated that he had dropped Curley Bill, there was blood on the ground, and some splattered on the leaves near the spot.

"You think the sonova bitch is alive?" Doc said.

"No. He took both barrels. They must have hauled him off to bury him."

They were quiet under the trees, near the still water of the spring. Doc looked thoughtfully at Wyatt.

"When they opened fire on us," Doc said, "you rode right in on them, 'stead of taking cover."

"I saw Curley Bill," Wyatt said.

"I done that, you'd have said I was a drunken fool," Doc said.

"Curley Bill shot my brother," Wyatt said.

"And you don't drink," Doc said.

Fifty-seven

Hooker's ranch was in the Sulfur Springs Valley near the San Simon River. There was a central fortified house and outbuildings, and grazing land spread out around the house to the horizon.

"Sierra Bonita," Wyatt said to Warren as they rode down the slow slope toward the main house. "Henry was a general in the war, came out here from back east after, found the best water around, and built a ranch on it."

"We going to be welcome?" Warren said.

"Henry's very hospitable," Wyatt said. He smiled. "And the cowboys been hitting his stock pretty hard."

"I'll be glad to get off this animal," Warren said. "Maybe sleep in a bed."

"Maybe have something but fried pork and biscuits for supper," Doc said.

The horses had been watered and fed and washed down and turned out to graze by two of Hooker's stable hands. The men had washed and changed clothes and sat on the wide front porch in the encroaching April night to drink before dinner.

"I'll have a little whiskey myself, Henry," Wyatt said.

Doc hooted.

"Watch out for this," he said. "Earp's having a drink. Be hell to pay for this."

Wyatt smiled and sipped at the whiskey. He still didn't like it, but he took pleasure in the warm spread of it through his chest and stomach.

Hooker sat with them and his foreman, Billy Whelan.

"Understand Behan's chasing you boys," Hooker said.

"Carefully," Wyatt said, "so's he won't actually catch us."

"I hear that Ringo's with him, and Pony Diehl, and Curley Bill."

"Curley Bill's not with him," Wyatt said.

Hooker looked at Wyatt thoughtfully for a moment.

"Well," he said, "whoever's with him, one of my drovers says they're coming along this way. Expect they'll show up here around midday tomorrow, looking for a meal."

"There won't be any trouble, Henry," Wyatt said. "I'll have my people out of here 'fore then."

"If you want trouble we'll back you," Hooker said. "I got fifty tough hands that can shoot."

"Behan won't fight," Wyatt said.

Doc poured himself another drink and gestured at Wyatt with the bottle. Wyatt shook his head. Doc laughed and put the bottle back on the table.

"Ringo will fight," Doc said.

"There's no reason to get Mr. Hooker's ranch shot up and maybe some of his hands hurt," Wyatt said.

"We could end it right here, Wyatt," Doc said. "Behan, Ringo, Pony Diehl, Ike Clanton, here altogether. We could finish the goddamned thing."

"No."

"You already got Brocius, why not clean the rest of it up."

Again Hooker looked at Wyatt without saying anything.

"No."

"You won't fight Behan, will you?" Doc said. "Because he used to be with Josie. You can't, can you?"

Wyatt turned his gaze on Doc for a long moment and Doc went quiet.

"In the morning," Wyatt said, "I want all of you up on the top of that hill." He pointed at the hill on the opposite side of the valley. "You can see in all directions, and if somebody wants to rush you, there's no cover from them on the hillside."

"What are you going to do?" Warren said.

"I'm going to stay here and see what Behan wants."

"He wants your fucking ass," Doc said. "You stay, I stay."

"No," Wyatt said.

"Who's going to cover your back?"

"We can arrange for that," Hooker said.

"At least lemme stay," Warren said. "I'm your brother."

"That's the plan," Wyatt said. "What's for supper?"

"Boiled beef tongue," Hooker said. "And some dry corn dumplings, and stewed gooseberries."

Doc finished the drink in one long swallow.

"Hell," Doc said, "I was hoping for fried pork and biscuits."

Fifty-eight

Behan and twelve men rode in at eleven the next morning. Three hours after, Wyatt's people were on the top of Hooker's bluff a half mile to the west. The horses were lathered, the men looked worn down. Men and animals were gray with dust. From the corner of the main building where he stood, Wyatt could see John Ringo behind Behan, and Pony Diehl, who Wyatt thought he might have seen in the bushes at the water hole. Ike Clanton hovered at the rear fringe of the horsemen. Hooker came out to meet them.

"Morning, John," Hooker said.

"We're tracking the Earps," Behan said. "Somebody said they was here."

Wyatt, wearing a Colt revolver, stepped around the corner of the hacienda and leaned against it. Behan glanced at him and looked quickly back at Hooker. Ringo saw him, and they looked at each other.

"There were a couple of Earps here, had dinner with me," Hooker said.

Billy Whelan, carrying a Winchester, stood a little behind Hooker and to his right. The horses in Behan's posse smelled water and were restlessly tossing their heads and shifting their feet.

"You were eating with murderers, then," Behan said, "and thieves."

"I've known Wyatt and Virgil a long time. They are men I'm proud to eat with."

"Would you say that if he wasn't here?" Behan said.

"I'd say it anytime somebody asked," Hooker said. "Look at what you're riding with, back shooters and cattle thieves."

Behan shook his head as if to deny the charge. He looked around the area, careful not to let his glance linger on Wyatt.

Wyatt still looked at Ringo. Ringo still looked back.

"Where's the rest of them, Henry?" Behan said. "They under cover someplace?"

"They left here this morning, right after breakfast."

"You sonova bitch," Ike Clanton shouted. "You know where they are."

Billy Whelan levered a round up into the chamber of his Winchester. The sound cut through the hot morning like a bell. Some others of Hooker's hands drifted into the yard and stood loosely scattered on all sides of the posse. Ringo paid them no attention. He looked silently at Wyatt, and Wyatt looked silently back.

"You can't ride into a gentleman's yard and call him a sonova bitch. You want trouble, let's get to it. Right now."

"No," Behan said and made a damping gesture. "No, no. We ain't here for trouble. We need to rest our horses," Behan said, "and get something to eat."

Wyatt and Ringo continued to look at each other.

"I'll sit at table with you, John," Hooker said. "But I won't eat with this rabble you brought with you. We'll set up a table for them in the yard."

As the Behan posse dismounted, Ringo edged his horse closer to Wyatt.

"You kill Curley Bill," Ringo said.

"I did," Wyatt said.

"Always knew it would turn out like this," Ringo said. "Now I'm going to have to kill you."

"If you can," Wyatt said.

Fifty-nine

In Denver at the foot of 17th Street in Union Station at track 7, Wyatt leaned with his arms folded against the marble wall and waited for Josie Marcus to arrive. She got off the train with her flowery suitcase, wearing a silk dress from San Francisco, her face a little flushed with excitement.

My God!

He took her bag with his left hand and opened his arms, and she seemed to jump into them, pressing herself against him.

My God!

He carried her suitcase in his right hand and held her hand with his left as they walked up 16th Street toward Larimer, to his hotel at the intersection. Josie talked. About the dress she was wearing and the train ride from San Francisco and the way the troubles in Tombstone were being written up in the San Francisco papers. Wyatt listened without exactly hearing what she said. He was listening to her voice, the way he might listen to music, and what he felt, as he heard the voice, made the content irrelevant. At the Broadwell Hotel, they had tea sent up to the room. They drank the tea as Wyatt listened to the music of her voice. Then the music modulated slightly.

"Is it over?" Josie said. "You and Johnny and the cowboys?"

"Almost," Wyatt said.

"*The Examiner* says you killed Curley Bill."

"Yes."

"And somebody named Cruz."

Wyatt nodded.

"It said in *The Chronicle* you killed at least four others."

"Papers say a lot of things."

Josie knew that the conversation should go in a different direction.

"Have you seen Johnny?"

"Behan?"

"Yes."

"Saw him at Hooker's ranch. Him and his posse."

"What happened?"

"What do you think happened, it being Johnny and all?"

Josie sipped some tea and paused to add sugar and sipped it again to see that she'd added enough.

"Nothing," she said.

Wyatt smiled.

"That's what happened," he said.

Josie knew better than to press the point, and she didn't want to spoil the moment, but she couldn't let it go.

"You didn't exactly answer my question."

"I said 'almost.' "

"Is it Ike Clanton?"

"Ike's all gas and liquor," Wyatt said. "He never shot any of us."

"So you don't care about Ike?"

"Somebody else will shoot him soon enough."

"Who, then?"

"Ringo."

"Why?" Josie said. "Was he involved with Morgan and Virgil?"

"Don't know," Wyatt said. "But he was close with Brocius. He said he'd kill me for shooting Bill."

"Maybe he was just talking," Josie said.

"No. John doesn't do that, except when he's drunk, and he wasn't drunk. Says something sober, he keeps his word."

"He won't find us," Josie said.

Wyatt was quiet. He drank the tea the way he drank coffee, holding the cup in both hands, his eyes very still, over the rim as he looked at her. His big revolver lay on the night table near the head of the bed. It looked so strange in the chintz and linen room.

"Well, he won't."

Wyatt nodded.

When the tea was gone, Josie bathed. When she was finished bathing, Josie came naked to the bed.

"You're going to go and find him, aren't you?" Josie said.

"Josie," Wyatt said, "you've been talking since you got here."

"Do you think it's time for me to stop?"

"I thought so a while back," Wyatt said and opened his arms.

Josie hesitated for a moment and then let it go, and put herself into his arms and closed her eyes and kissed him with her mouth open.

Sixty

Ringo was sitting against an oak tree in West Turkey Creek Canyon when Wyatt found him. There was blood on his forehead. His Winchester leaned on the tree beside him. He held a Colt .45 in his lap, and he was drinking whiskey from an open bottle.

Wyatt said, "John."

Ringo said, "Wyatt."

He was drunk. Wyatt could tell by the care with which Ringo spoke.

"You come back," Ringo said.

Wyatt nodded.

"Where's your horse?" Wyatt said.

"I fell off him a ways back," Ringo said. "Landed on my head. Horse run off while I was laying there."

"He wearing your boots?" Wyatt said.

Ringo shook his head seriously.

"I think I left them in a crib north of Sixth Street," he said.

Wyatt's horse, tied to a squat clump of mesquite, nuzzled at the inadequate grass while he waited for Wyatt. The inflexible July heat, six miles from Tombstone, was nearly claustrophobic.

"You come back to settle up?" Ringo said.

"Yes."

"Good."

The men were silent for a minute, feeling the hard press of the heat. Breathing the smell of it. Listening to it as if it were audible.

"You're drunk, John."

"My natural state," Ringo said. "Don't let it bother you."

"I don't mean to shoot you while you're drunk."

"I've shot a lot of men while I was drunk," Ringo said. "Hell, Wyatt, you wait until I'm sober, you'll never shoot me at all."

"We could let it go, John."

Ringo shook his head solemnly.

"No, Wyatt, we can't."

"Why?"

"We ain't the kind of men let things go."

They looked at each other. Ringo's eyes were soft as if they didn't focus well. Wyatt could hear the faint jingle of harness and the soft sound of the horse's mouth as the roan browsed on the meager grass.

Had that horse a long time.

"No, John, we're not."

Again they looked at each other in the reeking silence of the desert heat.

"But not today," Wyatt said. "I can't shoot a drunk sitting on his ass under a tree."

"No."

"Hell, John, I don't even remember how all this started."

"Sure you do, you stole Behan's girl."

Wyatt turned and started toward his horse.

"There'll be another time, John."

"No."

Wyatt kept walking.

"Don't make me shoot you in the back," Ringo said.

In the hammering stillness, Wyatt could hear the hammer being thumbed back on Ringo's Colt. Wyatt turned to his left side and down, pulling his own Colt as he moved. Ringo fired and missed, and Wyatt, from the ground and aiming upward, put a bullet into Ringo's brain.

The roan looked startled, jerked his head once against the reins that were tied to the mesquite, then went back to eating grass. Wyatt got to his feet and walked over to Ringo.

"So drunk he's got his gun belt on upside down," Wyatt said to the empty desert heat. He picked up the whiskey bottle and poured out what was left and hurled the bottle as far as he could into the scrub growth that littered the canyon floor. He heard the bottle shatter when it hit. He stood for another moment looking down at Ringo, who was still sitting against the tree. There was nothing in Ringo's face. Not death, not peace, not pain. Nothing. Wyatt nodded his head gently as he looked down at Ringo. Then he turned and untied his horse and mounted and rode away.

And I'd steal her again.

Epilogue

Wyatt was with Josie until he died, age eighty, in Los Angeles, on January 13, 1929 . . . Josie died in 1944 . . . They are buried beside each other in the Hills of Eternity Cemetery in Colma, California . . . Doc died of tuberculosis in Glenwood Springs, Colorado, on November 8, 1887. He was thirty-five . . . Johnny Behan died in Tucson, Arizona, on June 7, 1912 . . . Virgil died in October 1905, in Nevada, where he was serving as deputy sheriff of Esmeralda County. He was sixty-two . . . Warren Earp was shot to death by Johnny Boyett at age forty-five, in Wilcox, Arizona, in July 1900 . . . James Earp died at eighty-four in Los Angeles, on January 25, 1926 . . . Celia Ann Blaylock (Mattie Earp) died July 4, 1888, from an overdose of laudanum, in Pinal, Arizona . . . Ike Clanton was shot to death by a private detective named J. V. Brighton at Eagle Creek, Arizona, in 1887 . . . Bat Masterson died at his desk in the sports department of the *New York Morning Telegraph*, October 25, 1921 . . . Alvira Sullivan (Allie Earp) died on November 17, 1947, just short of her 100th birthday . . . Tombstone remains, shadowed by the Dragoon Mountains, twenty miles east of the San Pedro River . . . The mines are closed now . . . The primary business is tourism.